ANNIE'S ATTIC MYSTERIES®

The Unfinished Sonata

K.D. McCrite

Annie's
Attic

The Unfinished Sonata
Copyright © 2012 DRG.

The characters and events in this book are fictional, and any resemblance to actual persons or events is coincidental.

Library of Congress-in-Publication Data
The Unfinished Sonata / by K.D. McCrite
p. cm.
I. Title
                          2011917827

AnniesMysteries.com
800-282-6643
Annie's Attic Mysteries®
Series Creator: Stenhouse & Associates, Ridgefield, Connecticut
Series Editors: Ken and Janice Tate

10 11 12 13 14 | Printed in China | 10 9 8 7 6 5 4 3 2 1

— 1 —

By the time Annie Dawson ran through her front doorway, the telephone had stopped ringing. The answering
machine didn't catch a message before the caller hung up.

Annie had been on her knees most of that June morning,
weeding and mulching the flower beds that dotted the Grey
Gables landscape. With all the windows of the old Victorian
home wide open, the shrill summons of the telephone had
announced itself, loud and clear, to the outside world.

One thing Annie had developed in her adult life was a
weakness for a ringing telephone.

Maybe the urge to answer the phone as soon as possible
came from the years she and her late husband, Wayne, had
owned the Chevrolet dealership down in Texas. Back then,
a missed call could very well mean lost business. Or maybe
it was just a leftover instinct from her teenage years when
friends called day and night. Whatever the reason, she always hated it when she failed to reach the telephone before
a caller hung up. She reminded herself that she should take
the handset with her when she went outside.

A plaintive but soft meow at her feet caught her attention.

"Oh, Boots," she said to the gray, white-pawed cat, "did
I forget to feed you this morning? Surely not!"

Boots mewed again; she wasn't argumentative, not
even reproachful, but she was definitely beseeching. Annie

smiled, reached down, scooped up the fuzzy warm body, and then she picked up the handset and squinted at the miniscule screen.

"Cooper City, Arkansas," she read aloud. No name was listed to tell her who owned that unfamiliar number. "I don't know anyone in Arkansas," she told Boots, who merely blinked at her. "I didn't know there was such a place as Cooper City. But, if it's important, I suppose whoever called will call again."

Boots purred, but she failed to offer Annie any practical advice.

Annie sighed. Who in the world would be calling her from Arkansas? More than likely it was someone selling something. She grimaced. She got a lot of calls like that, selling everything from siding to candles to burial insurance. She refused to return the call. Why listen to a spiel if she didn't have to?

Toting Boots in both arms like the cat was a floppy rag doll, Annie was halfway to the kitchen when the phone rang again.

"Ah ha!" she said in triumph. "Boots, I knew they'd call back! Maybe it's not a sales representative. Maybe I won something."

She put the cat on the floor and hurried to answer the phone.

"Hey, Annie!" said a familiar voice.

"Alice!" she greeted her good friend from next door. "You didn't happen to make an unexpected trip to Arkansas in the last few hours and not tell me about it, did you?"

There was a brief silence, and then Alice said, "Annie?

Are you all right? What in the world are you talking about?"

Annie laughed. "I'm perfectly fine, and believe it or not, I have control of all my wits. It's just that someone in a place called Cooper City, Arkansas, called me a little bit ago, and I was outside. I hate missing phone calls, you know."

Alice chuckled. "I see. Well, I haven't taken any trips lately, unexpected or otherwise. In fact, I'm at home right this minute, and I wish you'd come over here as quickly as you can. I need help!"

A bit of alarm prickled along the hairs of Annie's arms. "Are you ill? Did you get hurt? Do you need me to call 9-1-1?"

"Oh, Annie!" Alice said, chortling. "You worry too much. What I need is for you to help me with this crochet pattern you suggested I do so I could learn to crochet. Specifically, I need you to show me how to crochet double treble stitches for this sampler afghan. You owe it to me; you really do. You talked me into making this thing. What is a double treble stitch? Will you please come over and demonstrate?"

"No need to whine or beg, my friend," Annie replied, smiling. "I'd be happy to give you a little assistance. I need a break from weeding that flower bed, anyway. What a back-breaking job gardening becomes as we get older! Or is it just me?"

"I wouldn't know anything about getting older. I plan to stay forty-something for the next forty or fifty years," Alice insisted.

"Sure—whatever you say, you young thing. Listen, I'll run upstairs and get cleaned up, and I'll be over. By the way, I still think it's great that you are broadening your skills by relearning how to crochet. Remember when Gram taught us the basics?"

She heard Alice snort in derision. "Skills, my foot! And you said it would be easy."

"It is!" Annie said stoutly. "Once you learn how to do it."

"Harrumph! So is building a house once you learn how to do it. All I can say is you better get over here and show me what to do before I put this whole thing aside and learn something simpler, like how to play the violin."

Annie laughed. "I'll clean up, change clothes, and be there in a few minutes. And I expect cookies."

"You might expect cookies, but you're going to get cream puffs."

"Oh. Well, whatever," Annie said.

Annie was halfway across her front lawn, walking the well-worn path from Grey Gables to the converted carriage house that Alice called home, when she heard the shrill sound of the telephone pour out of the open windows. She paused, torn between going on to Alice's or returning home. This time, however, the phone only rang twice, and then it fell silent. Annie frowned. It must have been a wrong number. She shrugged and continued on her way to the carriage house.

The carriage house had been built in the days when horse-drawn carriages were the chief mode of transportation in Stony Point. It looked so similar to the big house, that no one could dispute that the two were once a set. With its steep roofline, the weathervane on the turret, multipaned windows, and detailed gingerbread trim along the gables, the home's charm was its Victorian character and diminutive size. Annie's grandparents, Charles and Betsy Holden, had turned the old carriage house into living quarters, adding a porch that mirrored the one at Grey Gables, but scaled it down to match the smaller home's size. The façade gave a warm, elegant welcome to visitors as they approached. Betsy had sold the corner lot and the carriage house after Charlie's death. After Alice's divorce from John MacFarlane, it was with Betsy's help that she rented the carriage house from the new owner.

Alice greeted her at the front door, and Annie crossed into a small foyer. The high ceiling with its simple chandelier, white marble floor, and white beadboard walls gave a light and airy impression. Alice kept her decor in that entry to a minimum with an oval mirror on the wall and a small mahogany table with a bouquet of seasonal flowers. Today lilacs scented the air. Their beautiful lavender blooms and dark green leaves made such a pleasing contrast against the white walls and deep red mahogany wood that Annie stopped to enjoy the sight and the fragrance.

"I've been thinking about your 'mysterious' phone call, my friend," Alice said when Annie finally lifted her eyes from the lilacs. She added dryly, "As if I don't have anything else to think about, after that disastrous Divine Décor party last night. Anyway, I wanted to tell you that the last time I got an out-of-state phone call was three days ago. They wanted me to change my phone service provider. Thirty minutes later I still had not convinced them that I was uninterested in their offer."

"Oh my," Annie said.

"I think you're lucky you were outside and didn't have the handset with you. Otherwise, you would have had to listen to a spiel, or a plea, or some such thing."

"As a matter of fact," Annie said, "I heard the phone ring again as I was walking over. It only rang twice."

"Twice? That's odd."

"That's what I thought too," Annie said, "but maybe it was a wrong number."

"Yes, maybe. You know, you could do an Internet search on the phone number," Alice said. "That should tell you who's been calling."

"I hadn't thought about that!"

"Well, that's why you have me around. To remind you of things you don't think of," Alice said.

Annie laughed. "You know it!"

"Now, Annie, come with me." Alice grabbed her hand and led her to the kitchen table where she had arranged a plate of delectable-looking cream puffs. Also on the table sat her crochet disaster.

"Have some coffee and a cream puff, my dear friend," she pleaded, "and then tell me why my double treble stitch looks like a fuzzy fish worm. I promised everyone at the Hook and Needle Club I would have something to show them at the meeting tomorrow, and I absolutely refuse to show them that."

Alice indicated a chair. "Have a seat, and let me pour you some coffee. Or would you prefer tea?"

"Coffee is fine," Annie said, eyeing the delicate pastries on the table. "Coffee will accentuate the yumminess of those cream puffs. What's the filling this time?"

"Lemon."

Annie smiled brightly. "One of my favorites."

She took a pastry before Alice had finished pouring

the coffee and bit into it. The puff, with its sprinkling of powdered sugar, melted on her tongue and underscored the tangy breath of the lemon filling.

"Oh, Alice! You have a gift, my friend. A true gift."

Alice set a full cup in front of Annie and smiled, but the smile never reached her eyes. Annie put down the treat and tilted her head to study Alice.

"The trouble you're having with that stitch isn't enough to make you look that way," she said. "What's up?"

Alice sipped her coffee as if she were stalling for time.

"What is it, Alice?" Annie said empathetically. She briefly laid her hand on top of her friend's.

Alice sighed.

"I think I'm losing my business."

Annie blinked in surprise. "What makes you think that?"

"In the last several weeks my sales have fallen. Dramatically. Drastically."

This was bad news, indeed. Alice supported herself by giving Divine Décor and Princessa jewelry parties in customers' homes, and if she made no sales, she made no income.

"I'm so sorry to hear that," Annie said softly. "Do you know why your sales are going down?"

Alice shrugged.

"The overall economy, I guess. Business started dropping a few months ago, little by little, until now I'm not selling very much at all. At first it was the jewelry, and I thought, 'Well, I can make up that lost income by selling more Divine Décor.' But then those sales began to drop too. And last night was terrible! Only three people were at the party, and that included the homeowner. None of them bought a single thing. Not even a soap dish. Annie, I lost money on that one because I had the party gifts that I give away, and I always give the hostess a gift. The company doesn't provide those. The money for those items comes out of my pocket."

Annie gazed at her friend's sad face, and her heart ached. She remembered rough financial patches she and Wayne had weathered, and how frightening it had been when it seemed they might lose their income, their savings—maybe even their home. She and Wayne had had each other to lean on for support and encouragement, but Alice had no partner to shoulder the burden with her.

"One thing I've learned," Annie said, "is that no matter how bad things get, or how bleak the world looks, it won't stay that way forever." She reached over and took Alice's hand. "I suppose that sounds rather trite, doesn't it? It probably doesn't give you much comfort right now. It's just the way of the world. Change is constant."

Alice smiled, somewhat weakly. "You should know about change," she said.

"Indeed I do." Annie let a moment of melancholy sweep over her. "Losing Wayne, and then moving away from all that was familiar to me. Life without Gram as the anchor to keep me steady … yes, I have definitely been through changes."

Alice hung on hard to Annie's hand. "You've done it with such grace and strength, Annie," she said. "Your example gives me hope that I can weather this."

"You can do it, Alice!" Annie blinked back tears. "And thank you. You made my day."

The two friends looked at each other for a moment, and then Alice reached for the crochet work nearby, saying, "Now, if you can just help me with this thing."

Annie popped the last bite of her cream puff into her mouth and took the uneven beginning piece from Alice.

"I know it's a sampler," Alice huffed at the work Annie held. "I know it's just a learning piece, but I still want it to look right. Honestly, Annie, with this one it seems every stitch is a different size and shape, and I know they aren't supposed to be that way."

"Not to worry," Annie soothingly assured her friend. "I'll show you how it's done. If you'll just unravel that row, we'll start over."

She looked at the other three blocks Alice had lying on the table.

"See?" she said. "You've done the blocks of single, double, and treble stitches just fine. Even if they're a little uneven, they still look good. Once you're used to working with yarn, you'll learn to adjust the tension, and the stitches will come out even." She glanced at Alice's face. "And don't worry about it! Everyone who crochets has had this same problem at first with loose stitches and tight stitches. It just takes practice."

Annie reached into her tote bag, and then pulled out a hook and a new skein of yarn. Quickly she made a slip knot, crocheted a chain of ten stitches, turned, and crocheted a foundation row of eight stitches.

"Pull your chair right over here beside me, and then you can follow along."

Alice picked up her hook and yarn and watched intently

as Annie demonstrated a double treble stitch.

"It's really no more than just one loop after a treble stitch."

"Oh!" Alice brightened and nodded. "I see now! I think I got it. Do it again."

"You do it with me," said Annie.

Shifting her eyes back and forth as fast as a bank robber casing the joint, Alice watched Annie make the stitch one more time.

"Ah," she said. "Yarn over three times, and then you insert the hook into the next stitch."

"Yes," Annie said, nodding enthusiastically, "and it's the same as the treble stitch, but with one more loop on the hook. You work it just like the other stitches. You've been putting your hook into the stitch you just made, and then working it up. That's why it looks like a fuzzy worm."

Alice grinned. "I see! Annie, you're the best teacher in the world," she announced and whipped up a double treble stitch in her sampler, then did another. "Let's have another cream puff to celebrate!"

When Annie returned to Grey Gables a little later, richer by five cream puffs in a covered bowl inside her tote, along with the sampler afghan she was making as an encouragement for Alice, she was glad some of the light had returned to her friend's eyes. Alice's worry would return, of course, because that's what worry does, but Annie was going to put her own mind to work and try to come up with a way to help her friend get over this significant economic bump in the road.

She paused on the path to look at the flower bed. She'd

made good progress, but if she wanted to put in the new bedding plants tomorrow afternoon, she still had work to do. A glance at the gathering clouds encouraged her to hurry. The forecast promised rain for early evening, but sometimes forecasts were wrong.

Inside, Annie put the pastries in the refrigerator, and then she ran upstairs to shuck off her good jeans and white button-down shirt. She put on scruffy, somewhat ragged jeans; a T-shirt; and old canvas sneakers. A quick peek in the mirror showed a middle-aged woman with blond pulled-back hair; her nose and cheeks revealed the beginnings of a sunburn. Not exactly ready to pose for Vogue, but the woman in the mirror looked perfect for working with single-minded purpose in a garden.

She went downstairs, pulling on her gardening gloves. Halfway to the flower bed, she paused, and then she retraced her steps to retrieve the telephone. No more racing to the house only to be met with a dial tone. She glanced down at the screen and pulled up the log of caller numbers. The number from Cooper City, Arkansas, showed up three times. She stopped on the edge of the porch. No salesman or robocall would call that many times in one morning, so maybe it was an important call. Even so, Annie was reluctant to push the call-back button.

Alice's suggestion to do an online information search of the phone number echoed in her brain.

What a techno-world we live in, she thought, returning to the house and removing the gloves she'd just put on.

In the library she went to the small desk, opened her laptop and turned it on. It seemed to take a short eternity before it booted up, as it always did when she was eager to get information. Once Annie was online, she accessed her favorite search engine, found a favorable website that listed phone numbers, opened it and clicked the "Reverse Lookup" tab. At the prompt she typed in the mysterious ten digits.

She waited the blink of an eye before she had her answer. There it was, the name of the person who had been calling her.

The sight of the name caused her heart to skip a beat. It was someone she'd never forgotten. Someone she thought she would never hear from again.

2

nnie sat back weakly and stared at the computer screen. Grady Brooks. The name rose from her long-dead past like a youthful specter. Not frightening, certainly, but disquieting. Grady Brooks had proved nearly impossible to forget. For years, Annie had tried to move him out of her mind. She had succeeded, but it had not been easy. A person does not easily forget a first love, even when that love was as green and untried as new grass.

She grabbed the telephone, poised her finger over the return-call button, but paused. Then she pressed it. Immediately she pressed the "Off" button.

Annie sat and stared at the telephone while clouds continued to gather outside and blanket the sun. She contemplated memories as the first drops of rain pattered the ground. By the time she raised her eyes, an afternoon rain fell in a gentle shower that preempted all notions of a return to the flower gardens. She rushed to close the windows, shutting out the June rain.

Boots picked that moment to stroll into the room. She stood nearby, regarding Annie with unblinking green eyes. Sensing no objection to her company, she jumped confidently into Annie's lap. While Annie absently stroked the purring ball of fur, she lost herself in the summer of her fourteenth year.

She'd stayed at Aunt Susan's—her father's sister—that summer, while her parents were on a mission trip to Africa. Annie watched with considerable interest when the large moving van pulled up to the house next door. Soon a car parked in front of the house, and three people got out.

Annie had been sitting on the front porch of her aunt's house, nursing a cold glass of sweet tea, quietly observing. Behind her, Aunt Susan stood inside the house, just behind the screen door.

"Well, looks like the new neighbors have finally gotten here," she said. "And look there, Annie—a boy just about your age. Oh, isn't he cute!"

Annie distinctly remembered feeling her face flame. Aunt Susan was the kindest soul ever, but she had never learned to speak in a quiet voice. Annie scooted into the house where the boy couldn't see her. While Annie wasn't shy, she was at that postpubescent point between tomboy and young lady. She wasn't sure how she felt about boys, let alone how she felt about a new boy right next door.

As the summer passed, though, the two of them became friends, at first smiling and giving a quick wave across the yard, and then chatting a bit by the mailbox. Finally they sat together on Aunt Susan's stoop or on Grady's front-porch swing. He had turned sixteen that summer, and like her, he was an only child. His father's job had moved the family from Texarkana, and Grady wasn't sure he liked the change.

Annie realized she liked Grady. Very much. He had deep gray eyes that seemed to see beyond what most people saw, and he often spoke of serious subjects. He was soft-spoken and given to long silences. When she talked to him, he would really listen; Annie liked that. The boys she knew were too busy goofing off or talking about their own interests. Grady was different; she was proud to be his friend.

They went to see matinees at the theater once in a while and a couple of times had lunch at McDonald's. He never kissed Annie. He never held her hand. After a few weeks, she decided she must not be pretty enough or smart enough to attract him. She came to feel foolish and awkward.

Aunt Susan had taken to calling them "you two," as if they belonged together. By then, Annie realized she was merely Grady Brooks's friend and hoped he had never noticed how often she had gazed moony-eyed at him.

By the next time she stayed with Aunt Susan, Grady and his parents had moved to a larger house in another part of the city, and she never saw him again.

"This is ridiculous," she said, shaking herself loose from the memories. She had wasted so much time strolling along the path to yesterday that the rain had picked up and its drum on the roof jolted her back to present day. *No working in the flower beds now*, she thought a little grimly. But at least the rain could not stop her from cleaning the library.

It seemed to Annie that Grey Gables' cozy library would have attracted dust even if the room had been sealed, locked, and kept in cold storage. She fetched a feather duster for the tops of the books, lemon oil and a soft cloth for the wood, and a can of dusting spray for everything else.

The old house fairly burst with Betsy Holden's treasures, and the library seemed to hold the best of her collections. Intricate, hand-stitched tapestries hung on the walls, antique books with gold edges and leather bindings filled the bookshelves, and an old Victrola phonograph with a collection of 78-rpm records looked ready to fill the room with tunes from an era long past. In one corner, a tall three-point shelf held Gram's collection of music boxes.

Annie stood in the center of the room, her burden of cleaning supplies cradled in her arms as she stared at that shelf full of music boxes. Again memories flooded her mind.

She thought about other long-ago summer evenings in that very room, when the windows were open, and soft saltwater breezes blew the lace curtains inward. Gram would take down the music boxes, one at a time, wind the key on the back or bottom, and they would listen to the delicate music of each one, smiling and sometimes humming along.

Annie decided to dust the music boxes first and relive those evenings with Gram. Maybe by doing so she'd finally be able to consign thoughts of her first crush back to the far, dusky recesses of her mind where such memories belonged. In fact, she decided to make a party of it and went to the kitchen to brew a steaming, fragrant pot of mint tea. The dusting could wait.

Several minutes later, she settled into a small leather wing chair and sipped her tea while contemplating the corner shelf of music boxes and enjoying the anticipation of revisiting a part of the past that had nothing to do with adolescent boys with unforgettable, shining smiles.

In the meantime, Boots had curled herself into the deep corner of the old armchair. She was deeply asleep, and the whiffling sound of her soft feline snore added to the snug atmosphere of the library.

Annie finished her tea and then rested the thin blue

saucer and its matching cup on the table next to her chair. Finally picking up the dust cloth, she stood and approached the corner nook with a smile. She dusted the music boxes gently, studying each one intensely. She wound each key and listened to the tunes. She remembered one time when Alice had spent the night, and the two of them persuaded Gram to wind all the music boxes so they'd all play at the same time. The tinkling musical chaos they created had sent all three into fits of laughter. Maybe later Annie would call her friend over, and they'd do it again.

Annie stood on her tiptoes and reached for an intricately carved box that sat by itself on the top shelf. The largest in the collection, it rested on a crocheted doily. The gleaming, dark finish gave a pleasing contrast to the snowy white lace. It was the only one her grandmother never played. In fact, she rarely took it off the shelf except to clean the dust from its carvings.

Annie settled cross-legged on the floor and cradled the heavy music box on her lap, gently wiping the dust off of every inch. Try as she might, Annie could not remember why Gram neglected to play this particular music box for her. She ran her fingertips over the carvings and examined the thick English roses intertwined with curls of ivy. On the lid, two tiny lovebirds sat head to head on a branch, forming a heart. She opened the top, but rather than seeing a metal cylinder that played music, she saw a small wooden partition, as if the box had been designed to double as a keepsakes casket or jewelry box. But no keepsakes graced the interior.

Annie explored the underside with her fingers. She found the key, and tried to wind it, but it refused to move. Very carefully, she turned the heavy box upside down. There was the key—made of tarnished brass—solid and unmoving, though she jiggled and tapped it, willing it to wind.

So this is why Gram never played your music for me. Annie sighed and started to turn the box right-side up, but paused when she heard something rustle inside. Gently she shook it, hearing the sound again. It had a broken part, undoubtedly. No wonder the music wouldn't play—and it was the prettiest of all the boxes too.

Regretfully, Annie finished wiping away the dust from it and then got to her feet to return the music box to the high shelf. Once again she paused.

It's too pretty to keep on that shelf where no one can see it, she thought.

She could use it in the bedroom for trinkets, or even just for display in the living room. Such a beautiful box must have played beautiful music. It was too bad she would never hear it.

"But why not?" she asked herself suddenly. The sound of her voice awakened Boots, who popped open one eye to look at her.

Stony Point, Maine, with all its antique stores and clever craftsmen, surely had someone who could help her. It wasn't as if Annie lived on the moon or under the sea.

I'll just get the music box repaired, she thought.

Later, after a light supper and a long, soothing bath, Annie lay in bed, comfortably drowsy—until Grady Brooks edged his way back into her mind. She had a difficult time shoving the old days out of her thoughts until sleep finally pushed them away.

— 3 —

The next morning dawned sunny and warm, and it found Annie walking the seaside near Grey Gables. The Atlantic Ocean gleamed rosy and glittered silver. Annie paused to watch the unending reach and retreat of the waves. A night filled with bittersweet memories and half-remembered dreams had left her pensive and as restless as the sea.

Thoughts of her life with Wayne resurfaced. She and Grady had been little more than kids when they knew each other, but Wayne—who was never far from her mind—had been the love of her life. A massive coronary had taken him from her far too early. In her heart and mind she still longed for him; her arms still ached to hold him.

There had been few men in her life since Wayne's death. Ian Butler, Stony Point's mayor, had shown romantic interest, and they had gone out to dinner a few times. He was a man who could, if she wasn't careful, make her heart skip a beat from just one look into his beautiful brown eyes. But she was careful. Annie diligently kept their relationship casual, and nothing more. Their friendship was a warm, easy one.

She turned and retraced her steps toward the house.

It was Tuesday, and that meant the Hook and Needle Club would be meeting later that morning at A Stitch in

Time. Annie anticipated the meeting with joy and excitement. She needed some company and lively chatter to channel her thoughts from the past to the present. Besides, she really wanted to talk about the music box, and hoped one of the women could share some knowledge or insight about it.

A few minutes before eleven, dressed casually in khaki capris, a pale olive sleeveless blouse, and new bone sandals, Annie parked her trusty Malibu near the craft shop. She gathered the extra-large tote that contained her crochet project and the music box and went inside.

A chorus of voices rose to meet her the moment she stepped through the door, and she smiled gratefully to hear them.

"Good morning, ladies!" she sang out. "Isn't it a lovely day?"

"It is," agreed Stella Brickson. She was already busily knitting something thin and delicate. Her perfectly styled gray hair, lovely dark plum pantsuit, and lacy white blouse complemented her regal bearing. She looked her age, but she was an elegant and fashionable octogenarian. She gave Annie a sharp look as Annie sat down next to Alice. "What has made you so extra chipper today?"

"Just happy to be here, that's all." Annie laughed. "I enjoy seeing you ladies every week."

"Oh, so do I!" said Kate Stevens, the shop assistant. Dark-haired and dark-eyed, with a warm, sweet smile, Kate did not have an easy life. Being a divorced mom with a teenage daughter, she bore a lot of responsibilities, but her friendly nature and creative enthusiasm endeared her to anyone who came into the shop. "I keep pretty busy most of the time, and Vanessa is fun to spend time with. Of course, she's with her father often, so I'm alone quite a bit. To be perfectly honest, the Hook and Needle Club meeting is something I look forward to every week."

"I second that!" Peggy Carson agreed. "It's good to be around people I like, especially if I don't have to take their meal orders and bring their coffee."

The ladies shared a laugh with her.

"But you're everyone's favorite waitress," Annie pointed out with a grin.

Peggy giggled, and her dark blue eyes flashed merrily.

"Thanks, Annie. It's not that I don't like my job at The Cup & Saucer, because I do. I like it a lot, but it's just so nice to sit here and relax once a week."

The women murmured in agreement.

"Mary Beth doesn't get a chance to rest, though," Stella said, looking at A Stitch in Time's owner, who was assisting a customer choosing yarn colors. "She's always jumping up to answer the phone or to help a customer. It's a wonder she isn't more gray than she is."

"Kate too!" Peggy added. "Oh—I don't mean the gray part! I mean, she's busy during the meetings. It seems she is always straightening things on the shelves or adding things to the shelves or selling things from the shelves. Oh, and ringing up purchases on the cash register."

"But it's how we pay our bills," Kate said cheerfully, and in the chair next to Annie, Alice MacFarlane moved restlessly.

Annie shot a glance at her subdued friend. Alice smiled, but again the smile didn't reach her eyes. Annie knew Alice's financial worries would linger until the problem was solved.

"Ladies, you just have to see this!" Kate said with excitement. "I'm so happy with this new design. Tell me what you think!"

She came out from behind the counter carrying the cutest clutch purse Annie had ever seen. Kate loved purses, and probably had more in her collection than Annie had had in her lifetime.

"That is darling!" said Gwendolyn Palmer, leaning forward to get a closer look. Gwen was one of Stony Point's leading women and a local fashion maven. That day she wore a simple off-white dress with a cheery red belt and red sandals. Annie noticed Gwen's nail polish matched the belt and shoes. "Did you make it, Kate? Of course you did! You're just clever enough to do that."

"I want one of those purses!" said Peggy and Annie together. They looked at each other and laughed.

"I've already placed my order," Mary Beth Brock announced, joining the group at last. She patted her short salt-and-pepper hair, pretending to gloat. "But you ladies haven't seen everything yet. Show them, Kate."

Her cheeks pink with excitement—or maybe it was embarrassment from so much attention and praise—Kate unhooked the purse flap. It opened, and then opened again, revealing a different style of crochet and a new color of yarn. With a few deft motions, it had metamorphosed from a small clutch to a full-blown handbag large enough to carry most things women pack into purses. Kate had even added a colorful, contrasting strap.

Everyone applauded, but Mary Beth held up one hand.

"And that's not all."

"Pockets!" Kate declared. Pointing to each one, she sang, "Here a pocket, there a pocket. Everywhere a pocket!"

"You see!" Annie said loudly enough to be heard above the other voices. "This is why I love these meetings!" Every woman there agreed with unbridled enthusiasm. "Where else do we have this fellowship and great fun showing off our work?"

As she gazed fondly at the faces of her friends and listened to their chatter, she remembered how much she had wanted to be a part of this group when she first moved to Stony Point. Her grandmother had been one of the founding members, and she always took an active part. But fitting in had not been easy, in the club or in the small town. Being Betsy Holden's granddaughter guaranteed no favors from anyone, and in fact, it seemed perhaps more was expected from her than she could fulfill. But she continued to attend the meetings, throwing herself into the circle of crafting and involving herself in the town's events until, finally, she was a full-fledged, much loved member of the Hook and Needle Club and a respected citizen of Stony Point.

"Goodness!" Alice said. "You are such a craftswoman, Kate. And here I am, struggling to make simple sampler squares."

Annie glanced at her good friend again, a woman she'd known since they were both young teenagers. Alice had so many gifts that everyone else seemed to see, but that she herself couldn't recognize as special. An idea began to form in Annie's mind, a way to boost Alice's business and her confidence. For the time being, she shuffled the notion to the back of her thoughts and turned her full attention to

Mary Beth Brock, who was speaking to them as the leader of their club.

"With your permission, we have a fabulous new project for the summer," she said with a big smile. "But it starts this week." She held up one hand, squelching the rise of surprised comments. "Reverend Wallace called last night and asked if I thought the Hook and Needle Club would like to participate in the crafting part of the church day camp this summer. We would be teaching our skills to children and encouraging those who are creating art projects."

She paused, looking at the group expectantly.

"The floor is open for discussion and questions."

"How many days a week would we be doing this?" Stella said. "My summers are quite full, you know."

"Of course, I understand," Mary Beth said. "I think we all have a lot going on during the summer. However, we would rotate with other artists and crafters. Richard Gilbert with the local art guild, for instance, will be holding art classes. The church's Quilter Bees will also be participating. And you may choose the day and time you want to participate." She paused, and then added, "I hope you will all be as generous with your time as you can. I think this is a great way to serve the community and our next generation."

"Well, I think it's a lovely idea," Annie said. "I love sharing with children, and helping them discover the joy of being artistic."

"Yes," Alice agreed. "Remember when we worked with the high school? That was a great experience. I say we do it."

"Me too," said Peggy. "My Emily will be attending the day camp, and I'm sure she'd love it."

"Shall we make it unanimous then?" Mary Beth asked, sweeping her gaze across each woman. "By all the nods and smiles, I see we have agreed. I'll pass around this notebook. If you'll sign your name, and what day and time you'll be able to help, I'll pass it on to Reverend Wallace. Thank you, ladies!"

Annie and Alice chose Friday morning for their time with the kids.

With the business part of the meeting over, the women turned their attention to projects they brought with them. Peggy was quilting a small red, white, and blue wall hanging for the Legion Hall. Stella knitted on a lacy duvet cover while Gwen, the other knitter in the group, was making dishcloths as fast as she could turn them out. They would be given as tokens at one of her many fundraising events later in the year.

Annie began working on one of the squares for her sampler afghan. She nudged Alice, dipped her head toward Alice's tote, and then gave the half-finished square in her hand a little shake. Alice nodded, took a deep breath, seeming to make a visible effort to throw off her stress and concern. She smiled, and brought out her own sampler squares.

"Would you like to see my crochet progress?" she asked the group. Her voice was so light and so cheerful that no one would know she was worried unless they took time to look deeply into her blue eyes.

Annie was so happy that everyone praised Alice's efforts. Kate picked up the blue and white squares and smiled.

"This is the greatest way to learn," she told Alice. "Making a sampler will teach you so many different stitches, and then you'll be able to use what you've learned in other projects.

You've done a great job with these." She handed the squares back to Alice.

"Thank you, Kate! Coming from you, that means a lot. And Annie is a great teacher."

For a while, there was a small lull in conversation while knitting needles clicked, or thread whispered through fabric, or yarn slid almost silently from skein across hook. It was a moment that Annie marked and loved. She wanted to remember the peace of those few minutes. Then the phone rang, and Mary Beth went to answer it. An older woman came into the store, and Kate eagerly assisted her. When they both returned to the group, Annie cleared her throat.

"I have something to show y'all," she said.

"Uh oh," Peggy said, chuckling. "I've heard that tone of voice before, and it always piques my curiosity. Is it another mystery from the attic of Grey Gables?"

"You always pique our innate nosiness, Annie," Gwen said.

"Pardon me," Stella said with a sniff. "I refuse to call myself 'nosy.'" She paused, and with a smile, concluded, "But I will agree to being called 'curious.'"

Annie set aside her crocheting and reached into her tote bag.

"This did not come from the attic. It came from the library at Grey Gables."

The women stopped working on their various projects and eagerly watched her lift out and unwrap the box she had swaddled with such tender care in several layers of tissue paper.

"Oh!" they murmured in chorus, as she pushed aside the last of the wrappings to reveal the carved music box.

"That's beautiful!" Kate said. "May I see it?"

"Of course you may see it. All of you are free to examine it. In fact, I wish you would. And if you know anything about it, let me know." Annie handed it over to Kate, adding, "It's a little heavy."

As the music box passed from hand to hand, Annie said, "Gram has that wonderful collection in her library, you know. She played them at least once a week when I visited during the summer. This one, though, she never took down from the top shelf, and I never really paid much attention to it until the other day."

"I remember those days!" Alice said. "We'd sit on the window seat while Betsy wound them up and played them for us. My favorite was the small one with the mother-of-pearl shamrock. It played Danny Boy."

"Yes, that was a lovely one," Annie agreed. "This one, however," she said, as the music box made the circle and was now back in her hands, "is broken. Listen." She shook it and heard whatever was inside rustle softly. "Do any of you know someone who could repair it?"

"Maybe Dave Elliot at Elliot Brothers Jewelers would be able to fix it," Alice said, but Gwen shook her head.

"I rather doubt it," she said. "I think he only repairs watches and clocks. And his brother Dean doesn't do repairs of any kind. He's all sales and traveling to shows. Of course, it can't hurt to ask," she added with a smile. "Leave no stone unturned, I always say."

"My Wally might be able to help you, Annie," Peggy said. "You know how handy he is."

"Yes," Stella said, nodding. "Wally Carson is about the

best handyman Stony Point has. That fellow can do almost anything." She glanced up from her project to meet Peggy's eyes. "You're very lucky to be married to such a fine man."

Peggy beamed. "I know!"

Her pride in Wally caused Annie to miss Wayne more than ever, but she smiled at Peggy, so happy that her friend had such a great marriage.

"Can everyone be really quiet for a moment?" Mary Beth asked. "Shake the music box again, please, Annie."

Mary Beth cocked her head to one side, like a robin, and listened while Annie shook the box. She chewed the inside of her lower lip for a minute, her gaze thoughtful, and then she shook her head. "I don't know. Doesn't sound broken though, does it? It sounds more like something is in there."

"Oh, maybe it's a ring! Or a diamond bracelet," Alice said, all but clapping her hands in anticipation. "Wouldn't that be fabulous, Annie?"

Annie rattled the box again.

"I agree with you, Mary Beth," she said. "It doesn't really rattle like a broken part. It shifts, like ... like something soft, not metallic."

"Not a piece of hidden jewelry then," Alice said, making a face.

"I don't think so," Annie said, with an apologetic smile. "Sorry to burst your bubble, friend."

"Take it to Wally," Peggy said again. "He's at the library today, building some new shelving for the nonfiction section."

"I'll do that," Annie told her. "Thanks!"

~ 4 ~

After the meeting broke up and everyone went their separate ways, Annie said to Alice, "Let's have lunch at The Cup & Saucer."

Alice smiled brightly, but then the smile slid off her face as if someone had stolen it.

"I ... I'd like that, but maybe some other time," she said, looking away.

Annie was pretty sure she fully understood what had stolen that smile and had replaced it with worry. She treaded gently, because she did not want to wound her friend's pride with a display of charity or pity.

"Oh, please, Alice," Annie said. "Peggy said they have bread pudding today, and you know how I love bread pudding. If you'll save me the experience of having lunch alone, it'll be my treat. Please. For me? For old times' sake?"

Alice met her eyes, and Annie knew her friend saw right through the ploy, but she gave in.

"Old times' sake, eh? Well, OK then. But if I'm doing this huge favor for you, you absolutely must show me how to make the basket-weave stitch."

"The basket-weave stitch? I'll be happy to. That stitch gives so much texture to anything you make. But you need a little more practice with the basics before you learn it. Why the basket-weave?"

Alice shrugged. "Because it's pretty, and as you said, it adds texture. I can see that from the illustrations on the sampler pattern. I really want to learn to make it."

"And so you shall," Annie said, steering her toward the The Cup & Saucer, "when it's time for you learn it. In fact, by the time you're ready, you'll have mastered more of the craft, and it won't be so hard for you to learn."

Alice sighed with mock despair. "All right then. But if I'm having lunch with you, you must teach me when the time comes."

"You know I will," Annie laughed. "It's a deal."

The lunch crowd had dwindled somewhat by the time the duo walked into the cozy diner and found a booth near a sunny window.

Alice looked around. "This is such a sweet little place," she said. "Comfortable and cute, and it always smells good."

Annie took a deep breath, trying to detect the fragrance of cinnamon in the bread pudding.

"I sure hope they have some bread pudding left," she said, looking toward the kitchen.

"Didn't you have breakfast, Annie?"

She shook her head, a little shamefaced. "I know I should, but sometimes I just get busy ..."

"Well, the way you're carrying on about bread pudding, I thought maybe you'd skipped meals for the last three days."

Annie laughed.

"You have to admit, Alice, the bread pudding here is the best in this part of the world. It's almost as good as my Aunt Susan's." She smiled, and added, "Thank you so much for coming to lunch with me today. It's nice to treat ourselves this way from time to time."

"It is nice, isn't it? Thank you for inviting me, Annie."

The waitress brought menus, and as soon as she walked away, Alice leaned toward Annie, her eyes bright and curious.

"So, Annie?" She spoke as if they'd been discussing something significant moments ago.

"So … what?"

"I'm waiting."

Annie frowned slightly, giving Alice the full benefit of a confused look.

"What are you waiting for, besides lunch?"

Alice leaned back and huffed loudly.

"I know you, Annie. You went home yesterday and called that mysterious phone number, didn't you? What are they trying to sell you? Burial insurance? A condo on time-shares? Aluminum siding?"

Annie smiled and shook her head.

"I didn't call."

Alice raised one eyebrow, lifted one corner of her mouth and looked completely skeptical.

Annie put up one hand in a gesture of promise.

"I didn't call it," she said, "but I did look it up online."

She sipped her water, pretending to be nonchalant. She opened her menu, hoping Alice would take the hint, but figuring she wouldn't. And she didn't.

"Annie Dawson!" Alice said as sharp and sudden as a rifle shot. She leaned forward again, shaking her index finger six inches from Annie's nose. "Do not play games with me, girlie! Tell me right this instant who owns that phone number!"

Annie sucked in a deep breath, feeling a slight flush rise in her face.

"Someone I used to know," she murmured. "Hmm. Crab salad sounds good today, doesn't it? And lemonade." She hoped to distract her friend, but she should have known better. She wasn't surprised when Alice blew out an exasperated breath hard enough to breeze through Annie's hair.

"Who? Who did you use to know? When I hear terms like that I always suspect some sort of romantic interest."

Oh well, Annie thought, shaking her head and giving in a little. "It was just a boy who lived next door to my Aunt Susan down in Texas."

"I thought you said the call came from Cooper City, Arkansas."

"It did."

"Uh huh." Alice gazed at her steadily. "Why do I get this strong notion you aren't telling me everything?"

Annie watched a light flicker in her friend's eyes, and she wanted to quench it before Alice got wound up. Fortunately, the waitress returned right then, pencil poised above her pad. Annie smiled at her gratefully. She knew sooner or later, Alice was going to worm out every tidbit about Grady Brooks, but at least Annie still owned a few more moments of peace.

"Let's see. Everything looks so good," she said, stalling under the guise of perusing the menu.

"We'll both have crab salad and lemonade, and some bread pudding, if you have any left," Alice said.

Annie gaped at her when Alice snatched the menu from her fingers and handed both menus to the waitress.

"Hey!"

"You said you wanted crab salad and lemonade, Annie. Not less than a minute ago. And you've been whining for bread pudding since we were at A Stitch in Time."

"OK. All right, then. Yes," she said to the waitress. "Crab salad."

"And lemonade and bread pudding?"

She nodded. "And I wasn't whining," she told both women.

As soon as the laughing waitress left with their twin orders, Alice gave Annie a look that said she wasn't going to listen to any more nonsense. Anyone in the diner could see Alice was fairly bursting with curiosity, and Annie knew her friend was set to probe. But Annie had another trick up her sleeve, one that would work better than a phony study of the menu.

"So, what do you think might be inside that music box?" she asked.

The ploy worked as Alice jumped on the question with eagerness.

"I don't know. As we discussed at the meeting, it doesn't sound heavy, like jewelry or gold or a key, does it? But maybe money—the folding kind, of course. A letter? A postcard? Someone's report card?"

"Say! You have a fertile mind!" Annie said. "I hadn't thought of that. In fact, until we talked about it at the meeting I'd just assumed it was a broken part rattling around."

"You must admit it, Annie, we crafters are clever and wise." She tapped her temple with one finger and wiggled her eyebrows.

Annie laughed at her.

"Yes, so clever. So wise."

"And beautiful," Alice added, preening and fluffing her hair.

"Oh, absolutely and above all, beautiful. Both of us. But I sincerely doubt someone hid a report card in there."

They giggled like a couple of schoolgirls, and then Annie asked, "Alice, do you remember Gram ever trying to play that particular music box?"

Alice narrowed her eyes in thought, as the waitress returned with their lemonade.

"No," she said, slowly shaking her head. "Not that I recall. In fact, Annie, I don't even remember that music box. And it's so much larger than the others, you'd think it would stand out in my memory. Are you sure it was in the collection when we were girls?"

"Oh, I definitely remember it," Annie told her, "but Gram kept it on the highest shelf in the corner. She'd get it down when she was dusting, and she'd let me look at it, but she always held it while I looked, and then she'd put it away."

"Did you ever ask her to play it?"

Annie frowned. "I don't remember a specific time that I asked, but I'm sure I did. I mean, the way I loved music boxes, that would have been a logical thing to do, wouldn't it?"

"Yes, it would have. And I for one would very much like to know what's in there!" Alice said. "You'll tell me as soon as you find out, won't you?"

"Of course!" she sipped her lemonade. "In fact, I will tell everyone in the entire Hook and Needle Club, because I believe all the ladies would like to know."

"I bet I know what it is!" Alice said suddenly. "I bet it's a photograph."

"It might be."

"Or a newspaper clipping."

"That's possible. But why would any of those things be inside the music box?" Annie asked.

"To hide them, of course!" Alice's eyes sparkled. She loved fun and mystery more than anyone Annie knew. "Maybe the photograph is of an old love, or maybe it's a clipping about a murder that the murderer himself hid."

"Oh, for goodness sake!" Annie said, laughing. "More than likely it's just a piece of paper the maker or manufacturer enclosed that describes the music box and who made it. A hallmark, if you will."

Alice made a face.

"That is so logical that it's boring. Sometimes, Annie, you sure know how to take the fun out of things."

"Be that as it may, I'm taking it to Wally, anyway. A photograph or newspaper clipping should not be able to stop the key from turning."

Alice's eyes lit up again with a new idea. She leaned forward.

"But a big wad of cash might stop the whole thing from working," she said gleefully.

"Oh, Alice," Annie said, laughing harder. "I hardly think there's a big wad of cash in that music box. Anyway, the main thing is, I want to hear the music." The waitress approached with their plates. "Speaking of fun, here's our lunch—and our bread pudding!"

They began to eat, but Annie knew her friend would

soon return to the subject of the phone calls if Annie failed to keep her mind on other topics. Plus, what Annie had on her mind right then was far more important than any silly discussions about faded schoolgirl crushes.

"I have an idea," she said.

Alice looked up, her fork halfway to her lips.

"You are a creative woman, Annie. What's this new idea?"

"I want to have a huge party at Grey Gables."

Alice grinned, put down her fork, and leaned forward a little.

"Ooo! I like that idea!"

"I thought you would," Annie said.

"When do you want to have it?" Alice asked. "Who are you going to invite? What can I do to help?"

"I'm thinking we'll have it next weekend."

"Next weekend?"

Annie nodded. "I know that's cutting it close, time-wise, but that's all right. I want a good old-fashioned Texas cook-out, with barbecue, baked beans, coleslaw, corn on the cob … if we can get our hands on it this time of year. I'm going to invite a lot of people, Alice. A lot of people."

Alice almost clapped her hands in excitement.

Then Annie added, "And you're going to bring the jewelry and the home decor products."

Alice stared at her, the grin frozen in place. She didn't even blink.

"What?" she said, finally.

"I want to have a huge Princessa jewelry and Divine Décor party," Annie explained.

"When?"

"At the cookout, of course!"

Alice gulped and stared at Annie from wide, unblinking eyes.

"Both of them? At the same time? Together?"

"Something like that, yes."

Alice blinked one time. "But Annie!"

"But what?"

"I ... I ... Annie, I can't just throw two parties at once!"

Annie ate a forkful of her crab salad and calmly chewed it while Alice continued to gape at her.

"Why not?" she asked after a bit. She sipped her lemonade and calmly held her friend's gaze.

"Because! I can't sell two different product lines at the same time."

Annie set down her lemonade and dabbed her lips with a napkin.

"I fail to see why not. We can set up the Princessa jewelry line on the porch and the Divine Décor in the living room."

"Annie! This is the craziest idea I've ever heard. Get real!"

"I am getting real." Annie leaned forward. "Listen to me, Alice. You said attendance at the parties has dwindled, that sales have dropped dramatically. Didn't you tell me so just yesterday?"

Alice shifted uncomfortably in her seat, and Annie hated making her feel awkward, but she wanted to help get her friend back on her feet.

"Yes," Alice admitted, "my finances are pretty tight right now. But, Annie, you've hosted several parties for me before. How many can one person have?"

Annie shrugged. "What does it matter? The point is, I want to make this a big party. We'll invite not just other women in the area, but the men in their lives." She smiled. "You know most men will buy things for them, often when women won't buy it for themselves."

Alice nodded.

"OK. I'll grant you have a point. But, still … I just don't—"

"We'll have some good food, and some live music for entertainment, and you can demonstrate products."

"Annie, I am sure there is some rule about not selling both products at the same party."

Annie crimped her lips. "I doubt that!"

"It's probably considered conflict of interest or something."

"If you were trying to sell two competing brands, that might be something to consider, but wall hangings and earrings are not the same thing. In fact, the two products complement each other, if you really think about it. Each serves a decorative purpose, one personal and the other more domestic in nature."

Alice sipped her lemonade and seemed to consider this logic.

"Well," she said, noncommittally.

"Did you sign a contract that prohibits two parties at once?"

"I don't know. I don't remember any details that say anything like that."

"Well, there you go, then," Annie concluded. "Why don't you take a look at your contracts, check out the details and ease your mind?"

"Hmmm." Alice said. "All right, then. I'll find out."

"And if there is nothing to forbid such goings-on, we can have the two-for-one party."

Alice tapped a finger on the side of her glass and offered Annie a long, steady look as if waiting for clarification.

"Annie," she said finally, "why do you want to do this?"

"Why? Because I want to help you get your business going again, of course."

"I don't mean that. Well, it's just ... oh, I don't know what I mean, exactly."

"How about this: I'm doing it because we're friends, and I hate to see you under stress. I want to give you a helping hand, if I can. Throwing a huge barbecue with burgers and hot dogs is something I've wanted to do for a long time. This is a perfect opportunity."

"Annie, this is a lovely, generous gesture, but it's ... well, I mean ... Annie, are you sure?"

"Positive," Annie said firmly.

There was another brief pause, and then Alice said, teasing, "No lobster or clams?"

Annie shook her head.

"No seafood. This will be a Texas-comes-to-Maine cookout!"

"I see." Alice stared at nothing for a while, and then she smiled and met Annie's gaze with tearful eyes. "All right. And if there is nothing preventing two parties at once, then let's do it."

Annie added, "And if you can't sell but one product line at a time, we'll do that."

Alice reached out and squeezed Annie's hand.

"You're a great friend, Annie. Betsy would be so proud."

Annie could feel a grin nearly split her face. Those words were high praise.

"Thank you, Alice. Now, one more thing."

Alice sipped her lemonade, and then said, "And that is?"

"In the interest of your pocketbook, I'd like to incorporate a bake sale into this party."

Alice nearly choked on the drink, and her eyes grew bigger than ever.

"Annie, have you lost your wits? A Princessa jewelry party, a Divine Décor party, a barbecue, and a bake sale?"

"Why not? It'll be loads of fun. And you know your baked goods will sell like hotcakes. Forgive the pun."

Alice sat speechless, staring at Annie, her food and drink forgotten.

"It's not a long-term solution to your current dilemma, I know," Annie continued, "but it can help right now. It will give you some breathing room."

Alice nodded, her eyes growing watery once more.

"But, Annie—well, I'm just overwhelmed. I can't even eat my bread pudding."

Annie laughed softly. "I have never been so overwhelmed that I can't eat bread pudding."

Alice laughed with her, a little shaky and tearful. "I can't tell you how much it means to me that you're willing to do this. It will be a lot of work."

"Oh, not so much, if we organize it well. And it will be a lot of fun for everyone."

Even overwhelmed, Alice was able to eat her bread pudding with a big smile.

~ 5 ~

"When are you going to take the music box to Wally?"
Alice asked as they left The Cup & Saucer.

"I thought I would run by the library now, just for a minute to let him see if he thinks he can fix it. I don't want to take him away from his work. You want to tag along?"

"Sure!" Alice said with enthusiasm. "I'd like to pick up something to read."

"I wouldn't mind getting a book or two myself," Annie added as turned toward the library. "Although neither of us is going to have a lot of reading time for the next few days."

Alice fastened her seatbelt. "I like to read after I get into bed. Sometimes I go to bed really, really early so I can read for a long time. You ever do that?"

"Yes, quite often," Annie replied. "In fact, Wayne used to laugh at me for 'going to bed with the chickens' just so I could read in bed. Not that I did it every night back then, but you know, there is something so peaceful about snuggling down between smooth sheets, under a soft blanket, and opening a good book."

"Yes, with the lamplight all golden and soft, and the whole house quiet." Alice sighed. "It's a lovely way to spend the evening, even if it's not very exciting."

Annie laughed as she checked behind them before backing out of the parking space.

"I guess that depends on what you're reading! And anyway, at my age, I'd rather have quiet evenings than noisy, exciting ones."

"At your age!" Alice scoffed. "You sound older than my great-grandma. You really must stop saying things like that."

"Ah, I'm just feeling the passage of years, I guess," Annie sighed.

"Well, stop it!" Alice exclaimed. "You're only a couple of years older than me, for crying out loud, and you're almost making me feel old." Then she sighed. "When my business is going well, I don't often have the chance to spend a quiet night at home, reading. I hope sales pick up again soon. I hope I sell a lot at the party."

"You will," Annie encouraged her. "Times are rough right now, but I have faith in you, Alice."

"Thanks, Annie. I appreciate that. With a friend like you, I can't stay down for long."

The local library—white and imposing with its Greek-Revival architecture—beckoned readers with a promise of elegance and a lovely step into the past. At the front desk, a fifty-something woman looked up as Annie and Alice approached. The lenses of her oversized, white-framed glasses glinted from the sunlight pouring through the front windows.

"Good afternoon, ladies," she greeted with a smile. "How was the Hook and Needle Club meeting today?"

"Hello, Valerie," Annie said. "It was great, as usual."

"Yes, it would be great if you could get away from the library sometime and join us," Alice added.

Valerie Duffy was a busy reference librarian who seemed to be able to put her finger on any book or magazine that had just the information patrons needed to know. These days her skills had broadened to include the Internet and all things computer-related. She laughed at Alice's suggestion.

"I'd love to sit down and visit with you ladies while I finish that Shades-of-Green afghan I started about four years ago. Maybe when I have my vacation in a few months, I'll pop in at A Stitch in Time and add a few rows. I might get that afghan finished by the end of the decade." She laughed again, and then added, "You look like a couple of women with a mission. What can I help you find?"

"We're looking for a man," Alice said, wiggling her eyebrows wickedly.

"Oh?" Valerie said. "Well, if you find an extra one, pass him along my way, would you?"

She and Alice giggled like schoolgirls while Annie stood by, shaking her head and smiling. "Actually, we're looking for Wally Carson," she said.

"You do know he's married, right?" Valerie teased.

"Valerie!" Annie said.

All three women laughed, and then she pointed with her ballpoint pen toward the far end of the library. "You'll find Wally back in the nonfiction room. In fact, follow the sound of that saw."

"Thanks, Valerie," Annie said, still smiling as she and Alice walked away. They heeded Valerie's advice and trailed along the lovely old wood floor through shelves of books, following the sound of construction.

They found Wally examining the edge of a board he'd just cut. The smell of freshly sawed wood and a slight pall of dust lingered in the air. He looked up as they approached him.

"Why, Annie Dawson and Alice MacFarlane!" he said with a grin. "Fancy meeting you in a place like this."

"Hi, Wally," Annie said. "I see you're keeping busy."

He glanced at the built-in unit he was making for the library.

"Yes, it seems the library always needs more shelves, but these days and in this old place, space is hard to find. But I believe this built-in just fits the bill." He glanced curiously at the bag Annie held. "You going to fill that bag with books? When do busy ladies like the two of you have time to read?"

"I make the time to read, Wally," Annie said.

"So do I," Alice agreed. "Books are our friends. At least that's what the reading program tells kids in school."

He grinned.

"But I'm not going to fill this bag with books today," Annie said. "I have something in here I want to show you."

"Oh? What is it?" He set aside the board and dusted off his hands on the sides of his jeans.

Alice held the tote bag while Annie pulled out the music box. She unwrapped the tissue paper and handed the box to Wally. He took it from her and stared at it with awe and appreciation obvious on his face.

"What a beautiful piece of work!" he said. "Look at that carving!"

They walked to a small, nearby study table that had been shoved out of the way for Wally's work.

"I take it this is a jewelry box?" He set it down on the table and lifted the lid.

"A music box, actually, though I think that little compartment could hold trinkets or jewelry," Annie said. "The windup key is on the bottom of the box, but it doesn't wind. There is something inside. We can hear it sliding around. I don't think that whatever it is that's in there is stopping the movement, but something certainly is. Do you think you can get into the 'innards' of this music box, Wally?"

"Peggy was sure you could," Alice added. She grinned at him. "In fact, I believe she thinks you can leap tall buildings in a single bound."

"I left my cape at home today," Wally laughed. "My Peggy is a special lady, and I hate to disappoint her—and you—by admitting I'm merely human."

He examined the box, held it up eye-level and stared down every line and angle. Turning it over, he squinted at the smooth wood on the bottom and tested the stubborn key, and shook the box gently, listening to the sound inside. He turned it right-side up and traced the carvings with his fingertip. Finally he shook his head.

"I have to tell you, Annie," he said, "no matter what my lovely wife told you, I don't know a thing about music boxes. If I really were Superman with that X-ray vision of his, I'd tell you in a heartbeat whatever it is that's rustling around in there. I'm sorry." He finally handed the box back to her. "I know who might be able to help you, though. Mike, over at the hardware store."

"Mike Malone! Of course!" Alice said, nodding eagerly. "Good suggestion, Wally. Mike is so smart, always reading and publishing interesting tidbits in The Point."

Mike Malone not only ran the hardware store, he also printed the newspaper for Stony Point. Annie liked the owner of the hardware store, and she shared Alice's enthusiasm over his abilities, but she was disappointed that Wally couldn't put an end to her curiosity right then and there.

"If Mike can do it, I'll be happy to let him. To Malone's Hardware it is! Alice, are you coming with me?"

"Annie Dawson, you surely don't think I'd stop tagging along at this point?"

Wally chuckled and returned to the work they had interrupted.

"Good luck, ladies. Tell me what you find." He picked up the board and cast a teasing look over his shoulder. "And don't tell Peggy I'm not Superman."

"Our lips are sealed," Annie promised.

"Mum's the word," Alice agreed.

Before they left, they browsed the shelves for reading material. While Alice looked for a book in the romance section, Annie looked to see if there were any books about music boxes, but found none. She plucked a familiar old Agatha Christie novel off the mystery shelf.

In the car a few minutes later, Annie surreptitiously eyed the two selections in Alice's lap. She said nothing, but she hoped the books did nothing to fuel Alice's already overactive romantic imagination.

Mike Malone hailed both women as they walked into his hardware store. A quick glance around showed a store that had every tool, every paint color, every nail or screw that anyone could need—and yet the store was almost devoid of shoppers. Annie wondered if the same lag in customer activity affected Mike's business as it had Alice's. She fervently hoped the two of them had simply showed up at a time of day when Mike wasn't busy.

"Hi, Mike," she greeted, and Alice echoed it.

"Annie and Alice! Can I offer you ladies a cup of coffee? I just made a fresh pot."

Without waiting for a reply, he poured two Styrofoam cups full and handed one to each woman.

"How can I help today?"

Annie handed her coffee to Alice, put her tote bag on the counter and took out the music box. She had not wrapped it in tissue paper for the short drive to the hardware store.

"Can you help with this?"

He looked at the box Annie had set in front of him on the counter. She retrieved her cup from Alice.

"What do you have there? That's beautiful work." He started to pick it up, paused, and asked, "May I look at it?"

"Oh, yes, please do!" Annie said. "That's why I brought it in here. I was hoping you might be able to fix it, or tell me someone who can."

He frowned and picked it up.

"Fix it? What do you mean?"

"It's a music box that doesn't play."

His face cleared.

"Ah, I see." He turned the box over, and just like everyone else who had looked at the music box thus far, he tried to wind the key. "Huh! It doesn't move."

"Do you think you can open it and fix it, Mike?" Annie asked eagerly.

He jiggled the key once more, and then he took his reading glasses out of his pocket and settled them on his nose. He examined the box as closely as Wally had done and in almost the same way. Finally, he set it down on the counter again, ran the fingers of one hand through his thinning brown hair and tugged on his earlobe. He sighed heavily and shook his head.

"I don't see a way to get into the box at all unless it would be to take it apart. And that would destroy it."

"Tear it apart?" Annie plucked the box off the counter and held it closer to her chest like a child. "Oh, no, I don't want to do that!"

"I didn't think you'd want to," Mike said. "And it's probably an antique, isn't it? A collector's item?"

"I think it is, yes. Gram had it on her shelf at Grey Gables."

"I thought I heard something moving inside when I was turned it over a moment ago. Do you know what's in there?"

She shook her head. "I wish I knew."

"Why, Mike, it's a mystery, of course!" Alice said with a grin. "You know our Annie. She's a mystery magnet."

Mike chuckled. "She surely seems to be. Anyway, I wish I could help you, Annie. That's a fine piece of woodworking, and I'd hate to see it ruined."

"Me too!" Annie and Alice said in unison.

"Be sure to bring it by when and if you find someone to fix it, will you? I'd like to know what's moving around inside there. Odd."

"I'd be happy to, Mike," she told him, "and if you think of anyone who might be able to help, would you call me?"

They sipped coffee and chatted awhile until another customer finally came into the store.

"Excuse me, ladies," Mike said.

He took a couple of steps toward the customer, but

turned back to Annie and Alice for a moment.

"I just thought—a jeweler might know something," he said. "Clock makers and jewelers used to make and repair music boxes too, I think. Try Dave, over at Elliot Brothers Jewelers."

"That was my next stop," Annie told him, tossing the empty cup into a nearby trash can. "Thanks for your help, Mike."

"I don't think I was much help, but you're welcome. Talk to you later."

Back in the Malibu, Alice sighed from her place on the passenger's side. She took the music box out of the tote bag and ran her fingers across the carved birds on the top.

"I think this is called a wild-goose chase," she said. "Or maybe running around in circles."

"It's a little tedious, I suppose," Annie replied, "but I'm not giving up yet. I really would love to hear the music—and I'm so curious about whatever is inside."

"Me too! So ... to Elliot Brothers?"

"To Elliot Brothers!" Annie agreed, sounding like someone from an old adventure movie, and she started the car.

White-haired, thin, and dapper, Dave Elliot examined the box in much the same way everyone else had. He made all the same comments, gave the box an affectionate pat, and handed it back to Annie.

Shaking his head, he said, "I fix clocks and watches, but I can't do anything for you with this music box, Annie. I'm sorry. But I can tell you who's more likely to help you than anyone else I know: Papa Dexter over at Dexter Cove. He has that little antique shop, and I believe he just might have a collection of music boxes somewhere in all that stuff he's accumulated."

Annie had never heard of Papa Dexter or Dexter Cove, but Alice's exclamation of delight told her that her friend knew exactly whom David was talking about.

"Excellent idea!" Alice said. "I should have thought of him. Oh, Annie, you'll love the place. Papa Dexter is the only person I know who has more treasures than your grandmother."

Annie visualized a maze of miscellanea, piles of junk, and heaps of odds and ends. In spite of her eagerness to look inside the music box, she was growing weary of telling the story of the music box and hearing, "Sorry I can't help you." Besides, there was still flower gardening to do.

"Thanks for taking the time to look at the music box, and for your suggestion, Mr. Elliot," she said, shaking hands with the man. "Have a great afternoon."

She gathered up the music box, and led the way outside. Back inside the car, she said to Alice, "Let's go see this Papa Dexter fellow tomorrow, all right? I really need to do some gardening this afternoon."

Alice yawned. "Sounds good to me, Annie. I had such a restless night, and then I woke up far too early this morning, and I'm really tired right now. I don't have to do any gardening, but I do need to go through my Divine Décor and Princessa jewelry supplies. And I need to check my cupboards for baking supplies. I'm sure I'll need to make a trip to the market."

"I have plenty of eggs, flour, and sugar," Annie told her. "And I think I have a couple of pounds of butter in the freezer. You're welcome to all I have, because I'm not going to have time to do any baking for a little while."

"Great. I'll work up a list of what to bake, and then inventory the ingredients I have on hand. Cookies always sell really well at a bake sale. And cupcakes. And pies."

"You absolutely have to make—"

"Bread pudding?" Alice interrupted to ask with a friendly smirk. "Mine can't be compared to what they serve at The Cup & Saucer."

"I was going to say more of those delightful little cream puffs. But yes, bread pudding too, if you want to. I'll buy it all, of course."

Alice laughed. "Annie, you are so funny sometimes."

"Thanks. I guess."

She pulled into a parking space next to Alice's spiffy little Mustang near A Stitch in Time.

"Thanks for going with me this afternoon, Alice. How does about ten o'clock in the morning sound for going to see Mr. Dexter?"

"Sounds good to me. Have fun in your flower garden." She started to get out of Annie's car, but paused with one leg out and one in. "Oh, and just in case you're wondering, I have not forgotten about your mysterious caller. I expect to learn all the details. Soon." She grinned impishly, and then got out of the car.

Annie hadn't gotten away with a thing, after all, and she knew Alice could be relentless when she set her mind to it. She grimaced, sighed deeply, and drove home.

~ 6 ~

Annie had her hands in the dirt only a short time when a car pulled into her driveway. The driver honked two short beeps. She straightened and looked to see who had come calling on her. Her heart did a little quiver when she recognized the car of Stony Point's mayor, Ian Butler. She did not welcome that little quiver and forced it away.

Ian got out of the car, raised a hand in greeting and walked across the grass to where she was sitting, looking grubby and a little sweaty. Why did he have to catch her looking like a fashion reject?

"Hi there, Annie!" he said as he approached.

"Hi there yourself, Ian. Are you here to help me plant these impatiens, or would you rather plant the pentunias?"

He stood, fists on hips, and glowered, but with a definite twinkle in his eye.

"I show up here for a friendly visit, and you want to put me to work immediately," he said in mock outrage. "Good thing I wore my gardening garb."

She looked him up and down, noted the neat crispness in his long-sleeved white shirt, the thin, diagonal red stripe in his blue tie, and his immaculate dark blue slacks.

"I'd hate for you to get your wingtips dirty," she said finally, stripping off her grimy gardening gloves. "Here, give me a hand up, and we'll have a glass of sweet tea on the front porch, as if we were back home in Texas."

Ian extended his hand. Annie placed hers in it only long enough to heft her body into a standing position. The warmth of his touch both bothered and delighted her. Certainly she did not want to let her fingers linger against his any longer than necessary.

"One thing about growing older," she said, laughing, "you don't bounce up from the ground like you did when you were twenty. Knees are the first to go, I understand."

"Speak for yourself, ma'am," he said. "I'm as agile as ever. And this is not gray in my hair. It's just reflections of light."

"Hmm," she said, squinting at his silvery hair. "Yes, of course. I see that now. Thank you for pointing it out."

They laughed together and walked toward Grey Gables.

"What's this I've been hearing?" Ian asked as they went up the steps.

"Hearing?"

He nodded. "I've heard a rumor about you, Annie."

Annie felt uncomfortable, as if she'd done something wrong. The feeling puzzled her a little.

"He's just an old friend," she murmured, not meeting his eyes.

"What's that?" Ian said, cupping his ear. "You know, hearing is the next thing to go after limber knees and dark hair. But I guess it doesn't matter if I can't hear well if your music box doesn't play."

Heat flooded her face as Annie realized Ian wasn't asking about Grady. How would he have known about Grady anyway? How would he have found out since she'd told no one? She could hardly believe she was being so daft and shook her head.

Silly, silly woman, she scolded herself. She was more grateful than she could express that Ian had not mastered the art of mind reading. She paused on the path to the house and looked at Ian.

"Oh, you've heard about the music box, then? My, word does get around in this town."

Once her embarrassment faded, Annie realized how quickly the news of the music box had circulated through the citizens of Stony Point. She loved the small coastal town, but the ability of news to travel faster than the speed of light often left her feeling ambivalent and somewhat vulnerable.

"Word travels fast when someone has as many friends as you do, Annie. So tell me about this music box. Is it one of your grandmother's keepsakes?"

"I guess you could say that. It was in her collection, and it's such an interesting piece. I want to know more about it, and I really, really want to hear the music."

"I think that's perfectly understandable, Annie. Betsy had so many intriguing items in her home. I rather doubt there will be an end to all the interesting bits and pieces you'll find there."

"And nearly every one of them seems to have an interesting history behind it."

They resumed walking toward the house.

"Do you know anything about this music box—where it was made, or what it plays?"

"Not a thing. Alice and I are taking it to Papa Dexter tomorrow. David Elliot said he might know something about it, if it could be fixed, or at least opened. Do you know Papa Dexter?"

"I know him," he said, nodding. "I'd say if anyone can help you, it would be him. He has collected and maintained more antiques and artifacts than anyone I know."

"Have a seat, Ian," she said as they reached the porch. She swept a hand toward one of the old porch chairs. "I'll get us some tea."

She returned a few minutes later, with hair combed and a dash of lipstick added to her lips. On a tray she carried two glasses of ice tea and a plate of the small cream puffs Alice had sent home with her. Luckily she had restrained herself from gobbling them all down the moment she got home with them.

"Help yourself to one of these super cream puffs, Ian."

"Thanks, Annie. I will." With a delighted grin, he reached for one of the pastries. "These look like something your friend and neighbor might have made. Or did you?"

"No, I can't take the credit. Alice created them, and they are heavenly. Excuse me while I go get the music box."

Ian's eyes lit up when she brought the box out and handed it to him. He examined all sides carefully, as if it were made of glass, not wood.

"Beautiful chestnut, a rather rare wood these days, so I'm sure this is quite old," he said. "And that carving is exquisite."

"It is, isn't it? None of the other music boxes in Gram's collection are like this one. You're musical, Ian. Do you know anything about music boxes? Or anything about carving?"

Ian chuckled. "I'm not musical, Annie. I can sing a little, that's all," he told her, "and I only wish I knew how to carve like this. More than likely, if I tried, I'd carve my fingertips instead of the wood. Whoever created this box was a true artist."

"I agree." Annie sighed. "I just wish I knew how to get inside it. I'd love to hear the music, but I tell you, Ian, whatever is in there is making me more curious by the hour. Alice thinks it might be money."

"Peggy told me something was inside it. That just makes your mystery even more intriguing, doesn't it? Alice thinks it's money, eh?" He held it near his ear and shook it gingerly, and then he lowered it and gave her a grin. "Could be. Sounds like money to me."

"Really? You think it might be?"

"I don't know," he said, handing the box back to her. "It could be a letter. Or a will. Or a poem, or a story manuscript."

"For that matter it might be a page out of a 'wish book,'" Annie offered.

"Or a handkerchief," he suggested.

"Or a dried flower."

"Or an old scorecard," Ian countered.

"We're just so imaginative," Annie said with a laugh.

"Yes, we are!" he agreed.

"Think about it, Ian. How did whatever it is get in there to shuffle around loose that way?"

"Someone had to put it in, didn't they?"

"Yes! That's what has my curiosity in an uproar. It had to have been sealed inside deliberately. And that's why I don't think it's an old hankie, or recipe, or anything like that. I think it's something important."

"Something meant to stay hidden perhaps?"

She nodded. "Hidden or stashed, but probably not meant to be stowed away forever. I mean, it's not buried underground, after all."

"But, Annie, it just seems to me that if it was hidden or stashed, there must have been a reason of some significance."

"Undoubtedly. But that was a long time ago."

"Was it? Do you have any idea how long that music box has been on Betsy's shelf?"

"Since I was small. And no jokes about how long ago that has been!"

They shared a smile, but Annie sobered quickly when a new idea formed.

"Do you think someone might still want whatever is inside to stay hidden?"

Ian shrugged. "It's a possibility, Annie."

Annie did not like the turn of conversation.

"So you like those cream puffs, do you?"

He studied her a moment, and then nodded.

"Of course! They are fantastic!" He held one up, looked at it as if it were a jewel, and he was checking its facets in the light. "Alice really should open her own bakery," he said, biting into the puff.

"I'm so happy you feel that way, because there is something I want to do, and I need participation."

He shot a curious look as he chewed and raised one eyebrow.

"Care to enlighten me?"

"I'm going to throw a party, Ian. Actually a cookout, and I'm inviting everyone. Alice is going to display her jewelry and home decor, and—here's the part you're going to love— she's going to provide all manner of baked goods for sale. You will come, won't you?"

"I've never been to a home party for products, but yes,

of course! Especially if Alice will have plenty of cookies and cakes and all those artery-clogging goodies for sale. What does one do at these parties? Play games? Pin the Tail on the Donkey? Charades?"

"Actually, I haven't thought about games," Annie admitted.

"You might want to think about something like that, in case you need some sort of icebreaker. You know how some parties can be a little awkward at first."

"But surely not Pin the Tail on the Donkey!"

He laughed. "No. Not that. It's just a suggestion."

"Thanks, Ian. I'll keep it in mind. But truly, my focus simply has been to help Alice ... to offer a large place for her use, to sort of give her business a boost." She hoped Ian did not probe too far; one thing she didn't want was for Alice to think this was a "pity party" with customers showing up out of obligation or sympathy.

Ian gave her a sharp, measuring look, but then he nodded as if he understood what she did not say.

"Grey Gables is perfect for a large affair," he said. "Especially at this time of year when it's too late to be blustery and chilly, and before the weather gets hot."

"That's exactly what I thought!"

Ian popped another cream puff into his mouth. *They are nearly bite-size, after all,* Annie thought with a smile. She nearly laughed aloud at the expression of enjoyment on his face as he chewed.

"How about a band?" he asked. "Live music would be great! They could set up right here near the porch. Folks might even want to dance."

"That's what I thought too!" she said, "I love the idea.

Down home we'd have country music at one of these bar-
becues, but I'm thinking maybe something a little quieter,
eclectic maybe."

Ian nodded in agreement. Then he snapped his fingers
and sat straight up. "I know just the band. They're just
starting out, they're local, and most of all, they are good.
They call themselves the Nocturnal Loons, but don't let
that fool you. I think they'll play during daylight hours too.
They have a rather eclectic sound that appeals to just about
everyone. You may even know them: Jenny Simon, Rory
Flynn, and his brother, Billy.

"Oh, I know Jenny! She works at the flower shop. I'll
call her. Thanks, Ian!"

"You're welcome. I'm happy to help in any way I can."
He paused, and then added, "One more thing about this
party. I want to provide the hamburgers for grilling."

"Why, Ian, that's generous of you, but really—"

He held up one hand. "I provide the burgers, or I'm not
coming."

"Well, I certainly want you to attend, so you leave me
no choice. Please, bring the burgers. Thank you! And lawn
chairs, if you have any. I'm sure I don't have enough for
everyone."

"Will do."

They sat in comfortable, companionable silence for
a few minutes, and then Annie said, "We were saying a
few minutes ago that maybe whatever is in the music box
wasn't meant to be found. Do you think someone would
object to it being found after all this time? I mean, whatever that thing is, it's far too old to cause any sort of a stir

beyond interest or blatant curiosity."

Ian didn't answer for a moment.

"You're probably right, Annie," he said at last. "I guess I'm just … concerned that you don't get yourself in a position to be hurt by revealing someone's secret."

"Someone's secret? Like what?"

He shrugged.

"A skeleton in the closet, maybe." He sighed. "Or … oh, I don't know. I care about you, Annie. You know that. I guess I'm just trying to look out for you."

"Ian!" she murmured, looking away. One thing she did not want, at least right then—or anytime soon—was this kind, handsome man declaring any tender feelings for her. She had to derail his line of thought.

"Please don't worry," she said quickly, and then she jumped up. "Let me fill that tea glass."

Before he could respond, she had darted into the house to get the pitcher of tea. While she was in the kitchen, she took several molasses cookies from her cookie jar. They too, had been baked by Alice. If she could keep him focused on Alice's baked goods …

When she walked back out on the porch, Ian was standing near the top of the steps. He was gazing out toward the restless water of the ocean, and the breeze stirred his hair. Annie felt a pang knowing she probably had hurt his feelings—something she did not want to do.

"Here's more tea!" she said cheerfully. "And some of Alice's soft molasses cookies. That girl keeps me in treats."

Ian turned, and the smile he gave was half-hearted at best. She felt like kicking herself, but she knew it would be far crueler to encourage a more-than-friends relationship between them.

"Annie, thank you for the tea and the cream puffs, but I need to be going. Tartan needs his walk and his dinner."

She set down the tray and hid her discomfort.

"All right. Would you take some of these cookies with you? I can wrap up some ..."

He eyed the plate then shook his head. His smile never faltered.

"I'll buy some at the party." His smile slid away, and he looked into her eyes. She read his heart and dropped her gaze.

"See you later, Annie. Good luck at Papa Dexter's tomorrow. Let me know what you find out."

With that, he strode down the steps and to his car. Annie retreated into the house so she would not have to watch him drive away.

7

It was almost dark by the time Annie put the final plant in the ground and watered the area thoroughly. The growing season and the soil in Maine differed greatly from what she was accustomed to in Texas. She stood beside her new flower garden and offered a prayer that these tender new beginnings found root and thrived.

After a shower and light supper of soup and salad, she crocheted a couple more blocks for the sampler afghan while watching her favorite detective show on television, and then went to bed early.

After the full day she'd had, she expected to fall asleep quickly and deeply. Instead, her mind circled all the puzzles the last couple of days had created. Of course there was the music box—its origins, its creator, its contents. How had Gram come to own such a lovely and mysterious antique? Where had she found it? Or had it been a gift? Had she bought it somewhere? Had she known what lay inside, and was that the reason it had been on the highest shelf? Maybe Betsy Holden herself had hidden the object. But why? What secret would she want to hide from everyone so badly that she'd virtually sealed it in a wooden casket? Did Ian's concern have any basis in reality? If Annie exposed something someone wanted hidden, even many years later, would she be putting herself in danger—again? But that just seemed absurd, and she did her best to dismiss it from her mind.

Then Annie's mind jumped into other thoughts. Why had Grady Brooks, a man she had not seen, or barely thought of, in thirty years or more called her? How had he traced her to Stony Point? How did he know her married name? Why did he hang up before she could reach the phone? Why didn't he leave her a message? Why hadn't he called again?

Annie sat up and fluffed her pillows. She readjusted the bedclothes, and then she lay down again, wishing she could shut off her mind. No such luck.

Annie still had his number in her phone's memory. In fact, those digits all but flashed in front of her eyes as she lay in the dark. As she lay there, once again she batted around the idea of calling him. Maybe she would tomorrow.

But what would be the point of that? she asked herself. Why bring up old times and resurrect the memory of a silly schoolgirl crush? A crush she would be too embarrassed to admit to now. All that mooning after him and doe-eyed sideways glances at his handsome face made her writhe in discomfort just to think about it.

Unfortunately, this line of thinking brought her back to her conversation with Ian earlier that day. What would she do if Ian ever declared deeper feelings for her? How would she handle that situation?

Oh! All those thoughts kept exploding in her brain like bottle rockets, disrupting her rest, and giving her a headache.

She pulled the pillow over her head, trying to shut out the internal sounds of her questions, and at some point the sandman dragged Annie, figuratively screaming and kicking, to slumber land.

The telephone dragged her awake the next morning.

"Annie!" Alice's voice barked into the phone. "Where are you? I thought we were leaving at ten!"

Annie sat up fast. She looked at her alarm clock. 10:15! Good grief! How did it get to be that late, with her snoozing away like a fat bear in the dead of winter?

"I ... I'm, uh, running a little late. Give me a few more minutes, Alice, would you, please?"

"Sure. I'll keep the coffee simmering."

Annie believed she took the fastest shower in the history of shower-taking. She threw on a pair of jeans and a T-shirt so quickly it made her dizzy. She slapped on some lipstick, brushed a touch of mascara to her lashes, pulled her hair back in a cute blue clasp, thrust her feet into a pair of sandals and was out the door before she had time to think—or to fully wake up, for that matter.

"What happened to you? You're hardly ever late to anything!" Alice said the moment Annie stepped on her porch. She had been sitting in a small white rocker, waiting like a spider for the fly—at least in Annie's estimation.

"Sorry. I'm here now. Shall we go?"

"Where's the music box?" Alice asked as soon as she got in the Malibu. She turned to look in the backseat.

"The music box?" Annie asked, and Alice turned back around, gawking at her.

"As if you've never heard of such a thing! What is wrong with you this morning? You act as if you just woke up."

I did. Less the fifteen minutes ago. But Annie refused

to admit this aloud.

"Sorry," she said again. "I just walked right out of the house and left the music box behind. Won't take me a minute to run in and pick it up."

Inside Grey Gables, Boots sat in the middle of the floor and gave Annie the most baleful look a cat could bestow on a lesser being.

"I forgot to feed you!" Annie cried. "Oh, poor Boots!"

She ran to the kitchen, poured the cat a bowl of kibble and set it on the floor. Boots attacked her meal as if she had been starved for a week instead of going without a full bowl of her crunchy food for less than a few hours. She did not deign to offer a purr of gratitude. The indignant twitching of her tail as she ate told Annie everything she needed to know about the cat's state of mind.

She was back out on the porch and nearly to the steps when she remembered that she had forgotten the music box for the second time.

"Good grief," she muttered, going back inside. "I hope Alice didn't see that. She'll have me settled in Seaside Hills Assisted Living before the week is out if I keep this up."

"Sorry," she said as she opened the backseat door and carefully stowed the music box in the backseat. "Boots demanded her breakfast."

"Yes. Cats can be so unreasonable sometimes," Alice murmured, giving Annie a narrow gaze. "Are you all right?" she asked as Annie got behind the wheel.

"I'm fine," Annie assured her. "I just didn't get a very good rest last night, that's all."

They were on the highway when Alice asked, "Something bothering you, Annie? And don't bother saying no because I can see for myself that something is wrong. What's on your mind?"

Annie refused to engage in speculation about Grady or her precarious emotions concerning Ian, but she was more than willing to discuss the music box.

"Ian said something yesterday that has me, well, not worried exactly, but concerned."

"This sounds serious, Annie. What was it?"

Annie felt a feather of disquiet as she recalled Ian's concerns. She drew in a deep breath and asked, "Do you think we're doing the right thing by trying to get inside the music box?"

"Well, of course! Why would you think it's not the right thing?"

"Do you think whatever is inside it might be something that should remain secret and untouched?"

"Is that what Ian told you?" Alice shuddered. "That sounds a little dark and disturbing, don't you think?"

Annie nodded.

"I hardly think it's anything sinister, if that's even what he meant," Alice said after a few moments to think about it. "If it were something that had been hidden away in the last few years, perhaps Ian would have had a point. But that box has been in Betsy's possession since before either of us can remember." She paused. "Right?"

"Right."

"Whoever did hide it is long dead, I'm sure, or at least very old. Honestly, Annie, if that's what has kept you awake, please put it out of your mind."

Annie let her friend's words sink in and some relief trickled into her mind.

"I'm sure you're right, Alice. That's exactly what I've been telling myself. Still, Ian's caution makes sense, and he was worried."

"He cares about you, Annie. He likes you."

"I know." She did not want to discuss it.

"And you like him too, don't you?"

Annie did not reply to that. Instead, she asked, "How far away is Dexter Cove? Why haven't I heard of it before?"

Alice gave her an exasperated look, but she did not pursue the topic.

"Dexter Cove is not a town, if that's what you're thinking," Alice said. "It's just what Papa Dexter calls his place. It's about ten miles from here. I'll show you where to turn when we get close."

Dexter Cove turned out to be a small, weathered-gray house that overlooked the ocean. The view was similar to the view from Grey Gables, but more rugged and wild. The house looked like it had sprung from the shoreline after a shipwreck. Driftwood and shells, the hull of an old boat, and more miscellanea than Annie could catalog at first glance cluttered the area where grass might have once grown had it been allowed. Cluttered it was, but it was also tidy and somehow welcoming.

The door in the center stood wide open, and Annie could see that sunlight stretched a square across the stone floor inside.

Carrying the music box carefully, she followed Alice up the crushed shell pathway toward that open door. The wind blew briskly that close to the blue water, and it was cool and damp enough to raise chill bumps along her skin. The fragrance of coffee and bacon came through the doorway and windows that had been opened. It mingled pleasantly with the smell of the sea.

"Papa Dexter!" Alice called as they reached the front door. "Are you home?"

Annie heard the sound of a chair scraping against the floor, and a moment later a sturdy older man appeared in the door. His thick, white hair gleamed in the sunlight and beneath straight, silvery eyebrows, his bright blue eyes shone like sea glass. A neatly clipped white beard looked to have been on his chin and jawline all his adult life.

"Is that Alice MacFarlane standing at my threshold?" he asked, squinting into the bright daylight.

"It is!" Alice said merrily. "And I've brought a friend."

"Well, come in, come in!" the old man cried, smiling broadly and displaying a good set of teeth that time had made slightly dingy. "I'm just finishing a late breakfast. Would you ladies like something to eat?"

Alice declined for both of them as they entered the small home, but added, "If you have some extra coffee, we might take some of that."

"Indeed I do." He looked at Annie with a bit of curiosity. "And who might this lovely young woman be?"

"I'm Annie Dawson," she said, shaking his hand. "Did you happen to know Betsy Holden, Mr. Dexter? I'm her granddaughter."

He studied her face, and she saw recognition leap into his expression.

"Of course you are! It's in the eyes. And please, call me Papa. Everyone does." He swept his hand toward the ancient living room. "Please sit down, ladies, and I'll bring you some coffee. Sugar? Cream?"

"Just black," Annie said.

"A bit of sugar today, please," Alice added.

They sat on a sofa that might have been new in 1952. Its nubby mauve fabric was textured but not a bit threadbare. Other furniture was just as old, but in excellent condition. Like the outside, the house, though cluttered, seemed extremely clean.

Unusual paintings and wall hangings caught Annie's eye and interest until the man returned, a thick white mug of coffee in each hand.

"I'm not one for formality," he said, handing the mugs to each woman in turn, "but if you'd like something else to drink, or a bite to eat, just ask for it."

"Thank you," Annie said, taking the mug from him, "but this morning, I think I need some coffee before I can even think about food." She sipped the strong richness and felt a little stir of welcome energy.

The old man settled in a comfy-looking vintage armchair. The three of them chatted like old friends for a few minutes, talking about the weather and his business/hobby. Alice and Papa Dexter discussed the health of a mutual elderly friend in Ocean View Assisted Living.

Finally he turned to Annie, and looked at the wrapped music box on her lap.

"Well, now, I don't think you've come all the way from town just to sit around and have a cup of coffee with old Papa.

What do you have there?" He dipped his head to her package.

"It's something Gram had in her music box collection."

"Ah! One of Betsy's treasures, eh? A music box? Well, let's see what you have."

He leaned forward as she stripped away the papers. She handed the box to him.

"What can you tell me about this?"

He took it to a small table in the sunny front window. He studied it in the same way everyone else had, examined the carvings, gave the key a cursory jiggle, and finally looked up.

"Well, Miss Dawson—or is it Mrs. Dawson?"

"It's Mrs., Papa Dexter. I'm a widow."

He lifted his bushy silver eyebrows.

"You are much too young to be a widow, if you don't mind me saying," he said gently. "My condolences, my dear."

She blinked back a sudden and an unexpected sting of tears.

"Thank you. My husband—his name was Wayne—and I were very close. Losing him was … well, it was unexpected, to say the least, and extremely difficult."

"Indeed, I'm sure it was. I lost my dear Sally forty years ago, but there are days when it feels like just yesterday that she left me. We grieve for our loved ones and mourn our own solitary state."

Annie nodded. She gave him a small smile, but she did not trust herself to speak further without weeping. Papa Dexter seemed to recognize this and turned his attention to the music box.

"Mrs. Dawson, this is indeed a treasure. It is the first Malcolm Tyler box I've seen in at least thirty years, if not longer."

"Malcolm Tyler?" she repeated.

"Who's he?" Alice asked.

"He was an artist back in the 1920s," he said. "No one ever knew too much about him, even back then, other than that he was quite eccentric. Some say he was from Canada, some say New York state. Still others believe he was from Down East, but no one seems to know for sure. He wandered from place to place, living with whoever would take him in or sleeping in the open."

"I find that peculiar," Alice said.

"Many artists are very peculiar," Papa Dexter said. "It's part of the artistic temperament, I think."

"Well, yes, you have a point there," Alice agreed, "but how did he create his work if he was homeless?"

"Itinerant is the better word to describe him, I think, rather than homeless. People say he stayed in one place only long enough to make money to move on."

"Didn't he have any family?" Annie asked.

"Yes. Yes, he did. In fact, I read something about them a few years ago in an art magazine. I believe they are somewhere in New England, if I remember correctly. Let me think a minute." The old man was lost in thought for a while, and then he shook his head. He offered an apologetic smile.

"My memory is not what it used to be, I'm afraid, but the name of the place will come back to me. Probably about two in the morning." He laughed softly. "If you leave me your phone number, Mrs. Dawson, I'll call you when I remember where they live." His blue eyes twinkled. "Only I won't call you at 2:00 a.m., I promise." He looked at the music box again, and patted it gently. "Only a few of his music boxes exist. Some are in museums. There might be more, but they are privately owned. I don't think he made very many." He glanced at the two women. "There is something intriguing about some of Malcolm Tyler's boxes that most people do not realize, even some of the collectors."

More secrets? Annie and Alice exchanged an expectant look.

"What's that?" Annie asked.

"Yes, tell us, please," Alice said eagerly.

"They have hidden clasps and hinges, like secret doors in old mansions."

Annie could feel her eyes growing bigger. This might be a significant step in solving the puzzle about the music box.

"I'm sure that one does," she said eagerly, "because no one can find a way to get to the music cylinder inside."

"Yes," he said, nodding vigorously, "I'm sure too." He shook the box and whatever was inside slid back and forth. "Something is in there. But I assume you already know that."

"Yes! We've been chasing all over Stony Point trying to find someone who can get inside."

"Someone actually suggested we might have to break the box to get to it," Alice said with considerable indignation.

Papa Dexter looked alarmed. He all but clasped the music box to his chest as Annie had done when Mike mentioned breaking into it.

"No!" he nearly shouted. "You must never destroy this priceless piece of work."

"We'd never!" Annie and Alice said together, breathlessly. Then Annie looked at her friend and added, "I don't think Mike really meant for us to do that. He was just saying ..."

"I'm sure you're right, Annie," Alice said. She looked at Papa Dexter. "Do you think you can get inside it?"

"I believe I can. Now let me see if I can just find the hidden key. Usually they are beneath the wing of a butterfly."

"Oh?" Annie said. "I never saw a butterfly in the carving." Of course there was a lot of carving, and it was possible she had missed it.

"Sometimes they are quite small," he said.

The women rose from the sofa and went to stand near him as he examined the music box more closely.

"Ah ha!" he said after a while. "There's the butterfly, ... and there's the hidden catch."

He pressed with his fingertip. Annie heard the defined sound of a release click, and the music box suddenly was in two parts. A nearly invisible seam had kept its secret all these years.

Papa Dexter gently unfastened the unseen clasp on either side and set the top portion of the music box aside, revealing the music cylinder. More importantly, it exposed at last the mysterious contents to the light of day.

8

"Well, now," said Papa, "there it is."

He lifted out a roll of paper, about seven inches long, tied with a scarlet silk ribbon.

"Ooo!" Alice gasped softly. "Annie, look! What do you think it is?"

"I don't know." She stared at the roll of paper. "It could be anything."

The old man smiled and tenderly offered it to her.

"You do the honors, Mrs. Dawson," he said.

Annie stretched out her hand, and Papa Dexter gently laid the roll in it. She delicately ran the fingertips of her left hand over the thick, cream-color paper. She touched the silk ribbon and traced the discolored edges of the roll. She lifted it to her nostrils and sniffed the fragrance of wood, and paper, and days of long ago.

"What is it?" Alice asked again.

"I don't know," Annie murmured.

Her fingers shook slightly from the excitement of the find and from anticipation to see what was written on the papers. She sank into the nearest chair and untied the silken bow. She paused and looked at her two companions. Alice was nearly beside herself with eagerness, and in fact, her fingers clenched and unclenched as if she planned the snatch the roll out of Annie's hands any moment. Papa

Dexter watched, smiling, like an indulgent grandfather. He stroked his white beard.

"I feel as if I'm violating someone's trust," Annie said in a near whisper. "It's almost as if I'm invading someone else's home."

"Oh, for Pete's sake!" Alice cried. "Those papers have probably been in that music box for decades. It's not like you're opening someone's private mail."

Annie took a deep breath. "I know," she said, "but it still feels that way."

"Then let me open it!" Alice said, reaching.

Annie pulled back and gave her friend a reproachful look.

"I will open it. I'm just saying …"

"Indeed," Papa Dexter said, "I understand how you feel, Mrs. Dawson. Believe me, I have felt the same way many times over the years. In fact, one time I found in an old dresser an entire stack of the steamiest love letters you can imagine. Those letters had been written in the 1880s, a hundred years before I laid eyes on them. I was conflicted for a little while, but did I read them? Yes, I did! It drew me close to a star-crossed young couple and helped me to understand that we humans are the same, no matter what century we live in."

"What else could you have done other than read them?" Alice said. "Shred them, burn them—use them for lining the bottom of a birdcage? What kind of resolution would that have been? I think it was far more honorable to read them." She turned to Annie. "Come on, Annie. Let's see what's written on those papers. Maybe you're holding a cache of steamy love letters too."

"It might be nothing more than a laundry list or some recipes," Papa Dexter added.

"Tucked away in a music box?" Alice said.

He shrugged and smiled. "Old family recipes with secret ingredients, maybe."

Annie hesitated only a moment longer, and then took a deep breath and gently pulled one end of the ribbon. As it opened and fell away, the pages loosened. With Alice virtually breathing down her neck and Papa Dexter watching with his bright blue eyes, Annie unrolled the paper.

As the paper unrolled, the notes and lines of a musical score revealed themselves.

"It's a song!" Annie murmured. "A handwritten musical score."

At the top of the score was written in antiquated penmanship, "For Olivia." As she continued to unroll the music, she saw it was one long page, folded into several sections. The notes ended in the middle of page four.

"Rats!" Alice said with blatant disgust. She flopped back down on the sofa. "I was hoping it was something interesting."

"You don't like music, Alice?" Papa Dexter asked.

"I like it well enough, but I was hoping that," she waved a hand toward the pages in Annie's hands, "was something significant. Old money. A treasure map. A letter written by Abraham Lincoln."

"I see," the old man said with a smile. "But what if this is a piece of undiscovered music by—oh, I don't know—Rachmaninoff, perhaps."

"Mozart?" Alice asked eagerly, sitting up.

Papa Dexter chuckled. "Oh, I hardly think so. Someone

more contemporary. Gershwin, perhaps. Or Porter. Maybe Kern or Berlin. Someone during the earlier part of the twentieth century when Malcolm Tyler built these music boxes."

"Oh! Annie, is it?" By that time Alice was bolt upright on the sofa and had fixed her bright-eyed eager gaze on her friend. "Did Gershwin write that music?"

Annie scanned the document. She shook her head.

"The only name written is 'Olivia' in the title. There is no composer's signature anywhere."

"Olivia, eh?" Papa Dexter said.

"Yes. Do you know who that might be?"

He shook his head. "Not without a last name, no. Is there a date?"

Annie looked and said, "No. Nothing. Just notes and the title."

She tried to keep the disappointment out of her voice, but it wasn't easy. She was not sure what she'd been hoping was hidden in the box, but a piece of music certainly was not it.

"I'm sure the historical society would like to have this," she said as she carefully rolled the pages. "I'll take it to Stella."

"By any chance do you mean Stella Brickson?" Papa Dexter said.

Annie smiled at the old man as she neatly tied the fragile ribbon.

"Yes. Do you know her?"

"I've … seen her around. Fine looking woman. And a sharp business head on her shoulders."

Annie and Alice exchanged a glance. Was there just a hint of hidden romance in Papa Dexter's tone, or had Annie imagined that softening of his face, the quiet more-than-a-little interest in his tone?

"Are you and Stella friends?" she asked.

He hesitated just a moment before shaking his head. "No, not really."

Again the two women looked at each other, and Annie plainly saw the light in Alice's eyes. Her friend obviously shared the same notions. But Annie respected the old man and didn't want to pry, especially since they'd only met that morning. She changed the subject.

"Papa Dexter, do you know how to fix the little apparatus so it will play music again?"

"I might be able to, Mrs. Dawson, if you'd like me to try."

She gave him a warm smile. "On one condition," she said.

"Oh?"

"That you call me 'Annie.'"

"I'll do it!" he said, returning her smile. He glanced at the music box. "If you'll trust me with this magnificent box for a few days, I'll see what I can do to fix the mechanism."

"Thank you so much! I think I like you, Papa Dexter."

"And the feeling is mutual, Annie."

Later, on their way back to Stony Point, Alice asked, "So you're going to take that piece of music to Stella? Do you think it's anything valuable?"

"I don't know," Annie replied, "but one thing I'm sure of, it surely has some historical value, if only because it's so old."

Alice wrinkled her nose. "I guess." She grabbed up her purse and took out a pen and notebook, saying, "I think we better talk about a guest list and menu for that party."

Annie forced her thoughts away from the music score

that now lay carefully on the backseat of her Malibu.

"Ian mentioned games. What do you think?"

"Games! At a party for adults?"

Annie shrugged. "It might be a good idea. Get people warmed up, entertained."

"So OK. We can at least think about it, but I'm not so sure people will want to play games."

"Music!" Annie said. "I nearly forgot about that! Ian mentioned a local band, the Nocturnal Loons. What do you think?"

"I think that's great! Games maybe, food, guests, music." Alice wrote in the notebook while they rode along. "Let's be sure to invite Papa Dexter. Maybe he and Stella will get together."

Annie slid her a sideways look.

"Tsk, tsk, Alice," she said. "Are you matchmaking?"

"Why not? Those two aren't getting any younger."

"Alice!" she said, and burst out laughing.

"Oh!" Alice exclaimed a minute later with considerable excitement. "I have the best idea ever!"

"And that is?" Annie said with a smile.

"What about that fellow from Cooper City, Arkansas? The one you don't seem to want to talk about. I think you should invite him!"

~ 9 ~

"Oh, Alice! What a crazy notion. Get real, please."

"I am getting real. You have his phone number, Annie. You could call and invite him!"

"Alice!"

"What?" Alice gave her a wide-eyed stare of faux innocence.

"Invite someone to come all the way from Arkansas?"

Alice smiled beatifically and said nothing.

"What's with you?" Annie asked. "Why are you so interested in everyone's love life all of a sudden?"

"It's not all of a sudden," Alice countered. "I just think if someone is interested in a certain someone, and that certain someone is interested back, or at least might be interested back, it's a nice thing to encourage that interest."

"Oh, good grief!" Annie all but rolled her eyes. "You don't know if anyone has any interest in anyone else. It's all in your head."

"Annie Dawson, you cannot tell me Papa Dexter didn't express interest in Stella. You saw and heard him as well as I did."

"That might be, but you don't have the least idea if she'd be interested in him."

"And you can't deny that hearing from an old boyfriend has not stirred some old feelings in you. You're human, after all. At least I think you are."

Annie sniffed, ignoring that last remark.

"All that business with Grady and me was a long time ago, and he was not an old boyfriend. We were kids. There is no interest, believe me. And besides all that, he hasn't called again, so there!"

"Huh!" Alice said grumpily. She folded her arms over her chest and stared out the car window.

After a while, she said, in an offhand way, "So that's his name, is it? Grady. This boy from a long time ago."

Annie paused, and then said, "Yes. Grady Brooks."

"Grady Brooks," Alice repeated. "Hmm. I like the sound of that. Sort of artistic and virile at the same time."

"Oh, good grief!" Annie groaned again. "Please turn down the flame of your imagination, will you?"

They rode in silence until they reached the city limits. At that point, Alice jerked, as if someone had poked her in the back.

"I know who he is!" she shouted so suddenly that Annie nearly drove off the road.

"Alice! My goodness!" she said.

"I remember!" Alice yelled. "Annie, I remember Grady Brooks. You came up to visit Betsy one summer and spent a good part of every day moaning and groaning about not getting to see him, or mooning and sighing about his beautiful gray eyes, his curly dark hair, or his soft deep voice. Oh yes! I remember now!"

Annie huffed loudly.

"Forget all about that, would you? I was fourteen years old, and it was a silly crush. To him, I was just the girl next door."

"Must not have been 'just the girl next door' if he remembers you after all these years and calls you."

"He has not called me," Annie said stiffly. "He dialed my phone number, but he did not talk to me, and he did not leave a message."

"Still."

"Still, nothing! He's just a boy from a long time ago, and there is nothing to it, and that's it. I wish you'd just drop it."

"But, Annie, if he's trying to get in touch with you after all these years—"

Annie sighed, loudly this time and with considerable exasperation.

"OK, OK," Alice said. "I was just trying to help."

"Help what?"

She shrugged. "Just help."

With great relief, Annie recognized the signs of her friend dropping the subject. Or so she believed. Alice proved her wrong.

"It's another mystery for you, Annie."

Annie waited, knowing Alice would continue this line of thought.

"This Grady Brooks wanting to get in touch with you after all this time. Let's say he isn't interested in romance ..."

"Yes, let's say that. Please, let's keep that in our minds, Alice!" Annie was beginning to feel twitchy. She hoped this conversation did not end in a heated quarrel.

Alice held up one hand. "Just hear me out. Let's say Grady is not interested in romance. Then that begs the question: Why did he call you after all these years? How many years has it been?"

"A long time," Annie replied crisply.

"Well, he wants something," Alice said, ignoring Annie's exasperation. "That much is obvious. But what is it that he does want? That, my dear friend, is the mystery."

"For all I know, he might be looking for me to ask if I know the whereabouts of a mutual friend, or to find out when Aunt Susan died," Annie told her. "Maybe he wants some information about missionary work. You know my parents were missionaries while I was growing up, and a lot of people have asked me about that. Truly, Alice, you are making a far bigger deal out of a mere phone call than you should."

Alice ignored this observation in favor of something more provocative.

"Maybe he wants a loan."

"A loan?" Annie squawked. "Why on earth … ?"

"Or maybe he's adopted and thinks you might know his birth parents."

"He's almost fifty! It's a little late in the day for that, don't you think?"

"Or maybe he has a deadly disease, and he's been deeply in love with you all these years and wants to make sure you know his true feelings …"

Gratefully, Annie pulled into Alice's driveway. She stepped on the brake with considerably more force than she intended.

"Will you *puh-leeze* just get all these wild and crazy—yes, *crazy*—notions and what-ifs out of your mind, Alice? You're going to drive yourself—and me—insane." She winced inwardly at the crabby tone in her voice. More gently, she added, "Besides, you need to spend your time coming up with the guest list and menu. Ian put in a request for cream puffs, by the way."

"And that's another thing!" Alice said. Her eyes still had that faraway expression of being lost in thought and totally oblivious to Annie's irritation.

"Be sure you bake plenty of them. I'll help." Annie hoped bringing the conversation back to the party would reorient Alice to their original topic.

A flicker passed over Alice's face. "What? Oh, no, that's OK. I'll make plenty. They're easy. I was just thinking about Ian and Grady, and them being rivals for your hand."

Annie had had enough. She forced a smile and calm demeanor, but it wasn't easy. In fact, it was almost impossible, and she was pretty sure her facial expression more resembled a gargoyle than a frustrated friend.

"Goodbye, Alice. I'll talk to you later."

Alice nodded and got out of the car. For the time being, she seemed content to be living in her own little world of romance and mystery.

"'Bye, Annie," she said absently as she closed the car door.

As for Annie, when she got back to Grey Gables she went straight to the medicine cabinet and got two aspirin. The conversation had given her a headache, and she was determined to dismiss Alice's foolish notions from her mind.

She fetched her plaid tote, her current work-in-progress, the cordless phone, and took them all out to the porch. The midafternoon sunshine was golden and warm, drawing the scent of fresh growth from the earth. The Atlantic offered its rolling ocean vista, and the cries and calls of seabirds.

In times of stress, as well as for simple relaxation, Annie enjoyed crocheting. While her yarn and hook worked in synchronicity to create a lovely piece that had not existed until she made it, she found herself unwinding. Prayer always came easily; crocheting always gave her a sense of meditation almost as quieting as being in church.

Annie sat in the old wicker rocker and took her crochet from the tote. Putting the chair in motion with a gentle shove from her foot, she leaned her head back and closed her eyes. For a while, she allowed her overdrawn brain to lie dormant while she absorbed the sound of the ocean, the quiet comfort of her home, the familiar feel of the hook in her fingers, and the soft heap of yarn resting in her lap. The soft outdoor air caressed her skin, and Annie soon found a calmer place within herself.

This is what life is, she thought. *This awareness of life, the sights and sounds and smells, the feel and taste of it. From time to time, it's necessary to let all else fall away and simply be.*

After a while, feeling more relaxed than she had in days, Annie opened her eyes, gazed out toward the ocean for a time, and then finally she picked up the yarn. Making the sampler afghan was such a lovely and simple project that she relaxed even more as she worked.

As she crocheted, plans for the party began to sort themselves into compartments in her brain. The menu presented no problem. Burgers, potato salad, baked beans, coleslaw. Iced tea and lemonade for drinks. She nixed the idea of games because she thought there would be no need for them. An outdoor event was much less structured and stiff than a formal indoor party, so she foresaw no awkward beginnings. In a little while she would call Jenny Simon to see if the Nocturnal Loons band could play for the party.

She wanted to invite as many people as possible. The guest list presented a problem only in that there really was not time to send invitations.

Decorations or not? she asked herself.

Annie gazed around her surroundings, studied the sweeping vista of the sea, the well-groomed lawn, and the flower beds.

"No decorations," she said aloud. "Nature provides all that we'll need."

There would be ample room to accommodate all of her guests, of course, but perhaps seating would present a problem. Ian had said he could bring some extra lawn chairs. In Texas, when she and Wayne would throw a barbecue, people brought lawn chairs. She saw no reason why her guests at a Texas cookout in Maine couldn't do the same.

If I'm going to throw a party next weekend, I'd better get busy inviting people, she thought. She had made significant progress on the sampler blocks while plans fell into place, but now she reluctantly stowed away the yarn and hook.

She went inside to put away the tote bag and get the phone book, a pen and paper, and a glass of tea. When she returned to the porch, she settled down in the chair once more, and wrote down names as fast as they came to her mind. She knew there would be more as time went on, and Alice would be bringing her a list too.

Annie picked up the telephone to dial the first name on her list. It was then she noticed that there was a missed call from that very morning while she had been at Papa Dexter's place. Her heart skipped a bit as she recognized the now familiar number and the location. But once again, Grady Brooks had not left a message.

Why on earth was he calling when he refused to leave any message? Forget the scenarios that Alice had offered for Annie's consideration. The situation was beginning to go from odd to uncomfortably weird, if not downright creepy, and Annie had reached her limit.

"Enough of this," she muttered. "I'll call him and find out what this is all about."

But some things had to have top priority. She would make the party-invitation calls first. Annie shoved all thoughts and feelings about Grady Brooks completely from her mind for the time being.

She did not need to consult the phone book for the first name on her list. She punched in the number to A Stitch in Time. Mary Beth answered on the second ring.

"How are you, Annie?" Mary Beth asked after they exchanged greetings. "What have you found out about the music box?"

"I found out the maker of the box was a man named Malcolm Tyler. Apparently it's a rare and valuable antique."

"Good for you!" Mary Beth said. "I was sure it must be. It's just so beautiful and unique. Tell us all about it Tuesday at the meeting. You know all the ladies will want to hear about it."

"I surely will. Plus, I found out more than just the fact that it's valuable. I have a lot to share with everyone, but I'm still chasing a mystery."

"Oh? There's more?" She could almost hear Mary Beth's

curiosity crackle through the phone line. "Anything you care to share a little early?"

Annie laughed. "I think I'll save it for Tuesday when I have a bit more information," she said. "I won't keep you on the telephone long, Mary Beth, because I know you're busy. But I did want to issue an invitation to a down-home Texas-style cookout at Grey Gables a week from Saturday."

"Annie! That sounds like such fun!"

Annie hesitated, then chose her words carefully as she added, "It's a combination barbecue/Divine Décor/Princessa jewelry/bake sale."

There was a moment's silence, and then Mary Beth laughed.

"Good grief! What in the world has made you decide to do something like that? And, Annie, I have to tell you," she lowered her voice, "I've bought all the jewelry and home decor that I need right now. I mean, I love Alice dearly, you know that, but I have attended so many of her home parties. ..."

"I understand, Mary Beth, but when is the last time you went to one?" Annie asked.

"Well, let me think." There was another brief pause, and then she said, "It was last summer, I believe. Yes, that was the last one, because I bought a door wreath of freesia and silk daisies, and I got it at a really good price because it was an end-of-season close-out."

"And the jewelry?"

"Oh, goodness. I believe it was before Christmas when I bought my niece a matching set of earrings and necklace."

"I see." Annie wondered if other members of the Hook and Needle Club had stopped attending Alice's parties too.

"Why do you want to know this, Annie? And what's with this bake-sale idea? What's the purpose?"

"Alice is going to make some of her famous baked goods for sale—"

"But I really don't ... well, Annie, isn't this rather ... peculiar? I mean, you're throwing a cookout, but it sounds to me more like it's a fundraiser for Alice MacFarlane."

Annie bit her lip. She did not want the party to be seen or thought of as a charity drive.

"Please, Mary Beth, don't say that to anyone else, especially to Alice."

"Annie?" Mary Beth's voice was so quiet Annie could barely hear her. "Is Alice having problems?"

"Oh, dear," Annie murmured, completely at a loss for words. She was not handling this situation with the delicacy and discretion she had intended.

"She is, isn't she? Why hasn't she let anyone know? Well, she wouldn't, would she? Always putting on a cheerful face! Oh, this is terrible! Poor Alice."

"Mary Beth, please understand. I did not mean to make this seem like a fundraiser. It's just that she needs ... well, her business has fallen off, and I'm just trying to help her get it started again. If you and the other Hook and Needle Club members could join in it would be great. But we must not let Alice believe for one minute that this is anything more than a boost for her business."

Once more, Mary Beth did not speak for a short space of time. Finally she cleared her throat and said, "I totally agree, Annie. The last thing I'd ever want to do would be to embarrass her. And I hate it that she's struggling. You can count on me to be at the cookout. In fact, I want to help. What can I bring?"

"You want to bring food?"

"Absolutely."

First Ian offering to bring the hamburgers and Mary Beth asking what she could contribute—Annie almost felt like she was back home where no one went to any party or dinner without toting an offering of some kind.

"How about you provide the lemonade? We're going to need gallons of it. And I mean gallons, because I'm inviting everyone I know."

"I'll bring it! How about if I bring chips too? Chips always go well at a barbecue, no matter what else you serve."

"That would be terrific, Mary Beth. Thank you!" Annie smiled as a small weight lifted from her shoulders with one less thing to do.

"Would you like to talk to Kate about the party? We don't have any customers in the store right this minute."

"I would. Thanks!"

As the afternoon wore on, faded, and gave over to twilight, Annie had called almost everyone she knew in Stony Point. Many of the people she called were at work, and she had to leave messages on voice mail or answering machines. Kate had recommended sending invitations on Facebook, but Annie had yet to set up an account on any social networking site.

"You're going to have to enter this new age, Annie," Kate had said in a teasing voice. "At least that's what Vanessa keeps telling me."

"I will someday," Annie had promised. "Right now, I have enough to do face-to-face."

Both women had laughed, but Annie wondered if she really was missing something. Maybe she should get someone to help her get started at some point. Kate's daughter, Vanessa, would be the right person to ask.

That night, Annie sat in her pajamas with a DVD in the machine, the remote control on the table beside her favorite chair and her sampler afghan project within arm's reach. The phone rang frequently with people returning her call or responding to invitations. Nearly everyone wanted to bring food, and Annie agreed. Her Texas cookout was turning into a barbecue potluck, and she figured nothing could be more fun than that.

She had her mouth half-full of grilled cheese sandwich when the telephone rang. She tapped the pause button to freeze Bringing Up Baby, the old Cary Grant movie she was watching, and picked up the phone. She glanced at the caller ID.

Caller unknown.

~ 10 ~

Annie swallowed her food half-chewed and felt it go down in a thick, painful lump. She pushed the talk button. "Hello?" she croaked, hoping the caller could understand her.

"Annie Spencer?"

She recognized that velvety baritone voice immediately.

"I used to be. It's Annie Dawson now. Is this Grady?"

A momentary silence, as if she had surprised him by knowing his identity.

"Yes, this is Grady Brooks. Do you remember me? I used to live next door to your Aunt Susan."

"Of course, I remember you," she managed to squeak. "Would you please hold on for just a moment?"

Before he had time to reply, she flung down the phone and fled to the kitchen where she gulped down enough water to sink a ship. At least it flushed down the sandwich, crumbs and all, from her throat and gave her a moment to compose herself.

Back in the living room, she sat down primly in the chair, brushed any stray toast crumbs from her pajamas, cleared her throat twice, and then picked up the telephone and said, "Forgive me, Grady. I had a small emergency."

"Oh? I hope I haven't called at a bad time."

"It's fine now," she said, still gasping a bit, but more from nerves than toast crumbs. "It's good to hear from you, Grady."

"It has been a long time, Annie."

His voice—deeper, more mature—still had the power to take her back to those languid summer days of her fourteenth year. Odd how that little shiver still ran up and down her backbone. *This can't be right,* she scolded herself. *You're not fourteen anymore.*

"Hey, you remember that night you heard the kitten under your aunt's front porch?"

She recalled it, immediately, and laughed softly at the vision of yellow and white fluff they had found.

"I haven't thought about that in years and years," she told him. "Peaches, that's what we named her, wasn't it?"

"Yes. Do you know that cat lived more than twenty years? She made a great companion for my mother."

"Twenty years? That's a long time."

"Yes, and she was spoiled every minute of it. Sometimes I think Mom fed her better than she fed Dad." He laughed.

She looked at Boots and wondered how old Gram's cat was and if she'd live to a ripe old age. But why were they talking about cats when they hadn't seen each other in more than thirty years?

Apparently Grady was thinking along the same lines. He said, "Annie, I've dialed your number a dozen times in the last few days."

"I know. But Grady, why haven't you waited long enough for me to answer, or left me a message? It's been a little … well, a little frightening, to be perfectly honest."

A small pause.

"Frightening? I'm so sorry, Annie. Frightening you was not my intention, believe me." He let out a deep breath.

"You'll never know how much courage it took me just to pick up the phone and dial your number. That first time, I was almost glad you didn't answer. And then when I dialed again, I was afraid you would answer, and I lost my nerve, so I hung up. And the other times ... well, I've never been very good at leaving messages on machines. I seem to say nothing but a lot of 'uhs' and 'ers' and 'hmms.'"

"But calling and hanging up numerous times probably wasn't the best. I almost thought I had a stalker." She immediately regretted the accusatory words. "I'm sorry, Grady," she said. "That sounded a little harsh, didn't it? Please forgive me. I've been on edge lately. Let's just say next time you call, please leave a message if I don't answer. Will you?"

"I surely will, Annie. My deepest apologies for causing you any discomfort, because that was not what I meant to do at all." He paused for a moment. "Am I forgiven? At least for old times' sake?"

The apology touched her.

"Of course you are," she said warmly. "Grady, it's so good to hear from you again. From the caller ID, I see you live in Arkansas now?"

"Yes. In the Ozark Mountains, in a little town called Cooper City. I'm the mayor here."

"Oh, are you?" Annie said. "Do you enjoy that?"

"Actually, yes I do. Our town is quite small, so it's a very relaxed administration I head.

"That's great. It sounds like a wonderful job. The mayor here in Stony Point is a good friend. He certainly seems to enjoy his work." She abruptly broke off, feeling a little peculiar to mention Ian to this man.

"Maybe I can meet him," Grady said with enthusiasm.

That seemed to Annie to be an extremely peculiar statement. Perhaps she misheard him.

"I beg your pardon?"

He laughed lightly. "I guess I should have told you that I'm in Portland."

"Maine or Oregon?"

He laughed harder.

"Oh, Annie. You're still a delight. Maine, of course. I just flew in a couple of hours ago. I'll be here a few days, and I'd like to come to Stony Point to see you before I go home, if that's OK."

She took in this information, tried to process it, but wasn't sure how she felt about seeing him. It was one thing to talk with the man on the telephone, but to see him face-to-face? Would he take one look at her and remember all those silly, doe-eyed gazes she'd given him? Would he remember the time she'd leaned into him, eyes closed, lips ready, thinking she was about to receive her first kiss when all he'd done was brush a ladybug from her hair? Even after all these years, her face burned at the memory.

"Of course, if you'd rather not, I understand," he said after her silence went on too long.

She mentally shook herself. She was a middle-aged grandmother, for goodness sake, not a blushing, silly teenager!

"It would be wonderful to see you again, Grady! My goodness, it's been so long. When are you coming?"

"Would this Saturday be all right?"

"This Saturday?"

"Yes. Unless it's inconvenient."

"Yes. Yes, of course," she said. "I mean, no. I mean, yes, Saturday is fine, and no, it's not inconvenient." Her face burned even hotter. She might be a grandmother, but she was still a dithering child at the moment. She took a deep breath and got hold of herself.

"Why don't you plan to come for dinner, Grady?"

There was a small silence from his end, and then he said, "Actually, Annie, I was hoping we could spend more than just a couple of hours together. What would you say to a picnic instead of dinner? You could show me the sights in your neck of the woods, and maybe we could just spend the day together. Unless you'd rather not."

Annie's mind whirled.

"A picnic sounds like fun," she said finally, "but I'm having a huge party next weekend, and I really must get things ready for that."

Again there was a silence that spoke volumes, and it gave Annie time to reassess her projects and her time. She planned to have a couple of women who owned a small house-cleaning business in town come to clean Grey Gables on Thursday, and since nearly everyone she'd invited had insisted on bringing food, the work she'd have to do on that end was cut back considerably. She told herself she had the party as well organized as she could get it. She knew she was just making excuses so she could find some pretext to hide behind. She knew she was being foolish, and was probably hurting Grady's feelings in the bargain.

"Actually," she said, "now that I rethink it, I believe it's all under control at this point. I see no reason why I can't spend this Saturday with an old friend, catching up."

"That's terrific, Annie!" he said. She heard the smile in his voice. "Tell me how to get to your house and what time you want me there, and I won't be late."

She gave him directions, and they settled on him arriving around ten o'clock Saturday morning. After chatting a bit longer, they said goodbye and hung up.

Annie leaned her head back and closed her eyes, sighing deeply. She was so tired, almost too tired to go to bed, but once again her mind was almost full of more details than she could sort. She offered a little prayer for guidance and peace. She lifted her head, picked up the remote control and resumed watching Cary Grant spar on the screen with Katharine Hepburn. She woke up later and went upstairs to bed, not even remembering if she watched the end of the movie.

The next morning, Alice came over with her own guest list. She and Annie sat at the kitchen table, drinking a pot of tea and nibbling fresh molasses cookies.

"Alice, I can't believe you aren't as big as a house the way you bake these luscious goodies all the time. These cookies make me think of Gram."

"They should," Alice said with a smile. "It's her recipe. And I keep busy, so I guess I work off those calories. Though I think I'd better start being more diligent about how many treats I eat." She patted her slim waistline.

Annie made a face at her.

"Well, you're slim and trim yourself," Alice said, "so don't look at me that way." She dipped her head to the list she'd brought with her. "Take a look at that."

Annie scanned the list of names and nodded. "I've

called most of these. I'll try to call the others today."

Alice sipped her tea and then said, "I have a good idea."

Annie raised one eyebrow. "Oh? About the party?"

"No. About that piece of music."

"What about it?" Annie asked.

"Well, don't you want to hear it? Don't you want to know what it sounds like?"

"I do," Annie admitted. "And I want to know who Olivia is too. And I want to know who wrote it, and why it was secreted away in that music box. I've just had ... other things on my mind."

Alice leaned forward. Curiosity sprouted out of her like antennae.

"What kind of things?"

Annie waved a dismissive hand. "Never mind. Tell me your idea about the musical score."

Alice squinted at her, obviously trying to read her mind, but Annie didn't want to discuss Grady Brooks's visit right then. She knew her friend well enough to know that Alice would dither on about him, making up romantic scenarios, forgetting all about the party, the music box, and the score they found inside it.

Annie smiled blandly and repeated, "Tell me your idea about the music."

"Well, I want to hear it. Don't you?"

"I seem to recall your extreme indifference to that particular song," Annie reminded her with a teasing smile.

"That's because I had my heart set on something really cool, like a wad of cash." She wiggled her eyebrows comically. "But having had time to ponder the find, I'm now ready to hear it played, and I know just the person to do it."

"And who might that be?" Annie sipped her tea and looked over the rim of her teacup at her friend.

"Jason."

"Stella's chauffeur Jason?"

"The one and only," Alice said. "He plays the piano."

"He does?"

Annie tried to imagine the chauffeur, who drove Stella Brickson around town in a ten-year-old Lincoln and seemed to be her right-hand man, as being musical.

"Oh, yes. I think he's probably pretty good. And Stella has that lovely baby grand piano in her home, you know."

"Then by all means, let's go see Jason!"

"Right now?"

"As soon as I get my purse."

Alice drove them to Stella's large red brick Georgian house. Immaculately kept hedges and flower beds greeted visitors who approached the front door via a broad, curving brick walkway.

Stella greeted them at the door. Wearing a simple lavender dress with a lace-edged white collar and thin belt, her every white hair in place, Stella was the quintessential image of Stony Point's leading lady.

"What a pleasant surprise," she said. "Please come in."

She led them from the foyer into a lovely little parlor/sitting room, something like one might see in a museum with its marble floor and shining chandeliers.

"Please sit down. May I get you some tea?"

"No, thank you, Stella, none for me," Annie said as they settled into two small, white fragile-looking chairs with seats upholstered in white and pink floral chintz.

Alice declined as well, saying, "We finished a pot of Earl Grey at Annie's just a few minutes ago."

Stella seated herself in a stiff-looking leather wing chair that had the appearance of being in that room since time began. The woman sat straight as a ramrod, crossed her feet at the ankles, folded her hands in her lap and looked at her callers expectantly. The smile she gave them was gracious but formal.

"You have a lovely home," Annie said, glancing at the white marble fireplace flanked by two huge Boston ferns.

"Thank you. It's quite comfortable, and it suits me well," Stella replied. Then she tilted her head a fraction and asked, "To what do I owe the honor of this visit?"

Annie felt a little taken aback. She was accustomed to the Southern way of doing things, where caller and host exchanged pleasantries and a little chitchat about weather or local interests before getting to the meat of a visit. But she smiled brightly and took the musical score from the large handbag she carried.

"This is what was inside the music box," she said, handing it to Stella.

Interest flashed across the older woman's features, chasing away the primness.

"So, obviously, you were able to figure out how to get inside," said Stella.

Annie nodded. "Papa Dexter was very helpful."

"Yes. Alex Dexter is rather gifted that way. I should have thought to recommend him to you at the meeting." She glanced down at the paper. "Such old, fragile paper," she murmured, as she settled reading glasses on her nose.

Annie watched as the thin, aged fingers, with their rosy pink polish and flashing rings, gently unrolled the score.

"Ah!" Stella said softly as she saw it. She looked at all four pages. "Music! How lovely. Look at those delicate handwritten notes. Their form is an art unto itself, isn't it?" She continued to study the pages, each one carefully, and then she came back to the first page. "Who is Olivia?"

She looked over her glasses at Annie, as if Annie knew the person.

"I don't know. I don't even know who wrote the music, or when it was written. There is no composer's name or date anywhere on the score."

Stella glanced over the pages again.

"I see that." Once more her gaze settled on Annie. "Have you played it? Is it good piece of music?"

"I wish I knew," Annie told her.

"That's one reason we came to you, Stella," Alice said.

"My dear, I don't read music very well. But then I'm sure you mean you came to see Jason, not me."

"Guilty as charged," Annie said with a smile. "We were hoping he might be persuaded to play it for us."

Stella gave the score one last look, and then rolled it gently and handed it back to Annie. She stood.

"And what's the second reason?" she asked.

"We're wondering if you think the score should be kept in a museum," Annie said.

Stella glanced at the rolled paper in Annie's hands and said, "It's my considered opinion that most old things of any value are better kept in a museum rather than thrust in someone's dresser drawer or housed in someone's basement."

Perhaps the words sounded harsher than Stella meant them. She had a brusque way of expressing herself. Annie and Alice glanced at each other.

"If you ladies will excuse me," Stella said, "I'll have Jason come in here. He's in the back garden."

After she left, Alice said, "Stella is hard to read sometimes, isn't she?"

"Oh, I think it's because she's of a different generation and social circle than most of us," Annie said. "Beneath that exterior, I believe she's really very sweet."

"You believe that, even though she gave you such a hard time when you first moved here?"

Annie smiled somewhat ruefully, remembering the cold reception Stella had given her. But as time passed, the history between Annie's grandmother and Stella came to light, and Stella's long-hidden fears and hurts surfaced. Time and understanding had undercut Stella's resentments until, finally, she was able to accept Annie as a member of the club and the community. However, Stella remained a cool, often formidable woman, and her friends knew this was just part and parcel of who she was.

"I think she's lovely," Annie said, "Prim and proper to the core, God bless her."

"You would say that!" Alice reached over and gave Annie a quick hug. "You are so kind, Annie. No wonder you have fellas hanging around in the wings."

"Alice! I have no such thing, and please do not say something like that where someone else could hear you and misunderstand. You know how gossip travels in this town."

Alice shrugged, but she didn't stop grinning.

A moment later they heard the crisp snap of Stella's shoe heels against the floor and the heavier tread of Jason's steps; then the two came into the room. Jason, tall and utterly masculine, with dark hair going gray, looked out of place in the frilly, feminine parlor, but he didn't act as if he felt alien in that room.

"Good morning, Annie, Alice," he said in cordial greeting. "Lovely day. I understand you have something to show me?"

"And I understand you can play the piano," Annie said, handing him the music. "Can you play this?"

"Careful!" Stella cautioned him as he took the roll. "That is very old."

"Yes, ma'am," he said, unrolling the delicate paper. His eyes lit up as he perused the score. "Wow! Where'd you find this?" he asked, lifting his gaze to Annie.

She told him about the music box, and then she filled him in on the roundabout search she and Alice had had up to that point.

"We have no idea who wrote it, or who Olivia is," Annie said, "but we were hoping you could play it for us. I understand you're quite good."

"My dear," Stella said, "he is extremely good. Let's go into the music room, shall we? Then Jason can play this mysterious piece of music for us."

"Well, ma'am," Jason said, looking first at one and then the other, "it's been a while since I've played the piano. I'm awfully rusty."

"Nonsense!" Stella said briskly. "Come along."

Jason handed the paper back to Annie and looked at his

hands. "I need to wash up. I never should have handled that old document with such dirty hands."

"Very well. We'll be waiting in the music room." Stella led the two friends into a bright, high-ceilinged, white room across the foyer where an ebony baby grand piano stood gleaming in the late morning light. Several small, elegant Victorian chairs had been arranged around the room, and Stella invited the women to sit.

"Are you coming to the cookout, Stella?" Alice asked.

The older woman toyed with the delicate pendant at her neck.

"Of course. I rarely miss a Stony Point function. But tell me, Annie. How does one dress for such an occasion? Casually, I assume?"

"Oh, my, yes! Jeans, T-shirts and sneakers are just fine."

A thoughtful look fell over Stella's refined features, and after a moment or two, she said, "I don't believe I have any jeans, T-shirts and sneakers."

"You just show up, Stella," Annie said warmly, "and dress the way you feel most comfortable. We want you to be there and to have fun."

"Thank you," the older woman said, smiling. "I'm looking forward to it." Then she asked, "I believe tomorrow is your day at the school, isn't it, Annie? Yours and Alice's, if I remember correctly."

A frisson of panic shot down Annie's back. She had all but forgotten the Hook and Needle Club project. "Yes, it is. What fun it will be to teach those children."

Stella looked skeptical. "If you can get them to sit still long enough, then more power to you. I'm not altogether convinced this project Mary Beth and Reverend Wallace cooked up was such a good idea."

"Sure it is!" Alice put in. "Why, this is something those kids will remember when they're as old as … as old as the rest of us. And Annie is a great teacher of crochet. I might have given up already if she hadn't been the one to guide me."

Stella gave Annie a speculative gaze. "You've inherited your grandmother's gift of crafting and teaching."

"I hope so. She was thorough, but so patient."

Jason walked into the room. He had done more than wash his hands; he had changed into neatly pressed slacks and a pale yellow polo shirt.

"Well, let's see about that composition," he said. Annie handed it to him, and he seated himself on the black bench.

"These pages are going to curl," he said as he unrolled the music score along the stand.

Stella got up and took him two small, leather-bound books from a table near the window. He positioned the books gently against the old paper to hold it open as Stella returned to her chair.

Jason flexed and stretched his fingers several times.

"As I said before, I'm a little rusty," he told them with a laugh. "Mrs. B, when was the last time I played? Christmas, wasn't it?"

"I believe so, yes." She glanced at her guests. "But that's not my fault. I try to get him to play for me quite often, but he's always got some excuse or other. Maybe I need to find old scores hidden in music boxes."

They all chuckled. Jason played a few scales and chords, studied the written notes spread before him, and then said,

"Well, here goes, ladies."

The piece started out slowly, sweet tones as fluid and light as moving air, giving Annie a sense of the touch of fingertips caressing her skin. As Jason continued, the music retained its soft quality but embodied a more robust sound—not lively or heavy, but strong. The tune found its way across the entire keyboard, coaxing the listener with higher, dreamier notes, and rewarding them with deeper, more powerful tones. It almost seemed to Annie that this was music she might hear in a dream—a dream of candlelight and romance.

Jason stopped playing abruptly.

They waited, but he did not continue.

"This composer obviously was influenced by Debussy," he said to the women over his shoulder. "The way his music seems to touch all your senses, it's almost poetic." He turned to glance at the women. "The person who wrote this piece has done the same thing, wouldn't you say?"

"Absolutely," Annie agreed fervently.

"It sent shivers all over me," Alice said. "Look!" She held out one arm to demonstrate the appreciative prickles along her skin.

"That's quite interesting," Stella said, "and I agree that it's an enchanting bit of music, but please finish the song, Jason."

"Yes, do. It's so lovely," Annie added.

"Sorry, Mrs. B, Annie. That's all there is."

They gaped at him.

"That's all?" Alice said, nearly shouting. "But ... how can that be all?"

Jason shrugged. "It simply stops right there at the end of the page. Perhaps the rest of it is elsewhere."

"You mean the piece of music that finishes the song is somewhere else?" Alice asked.

Jason nodded. "Or at least continues the sonata."

"But that's all that was in the music box," Annie cried. "Alice, I didn't see anything else in the music box, did you?"

"No. Nothing else. Oh, dear. What a shame."

They were silent a minute.

"I wonder if the rest of it is hidden in another music box," Annie said.

"Oh, no!" Alice said. "That would be awful."

"More awful than a composition that stops without ending?" Annie said.

Alice shook her head.

"It's a shame," said Stella.

"It's a tragedy," Jason added.

All four of them sighed.

"Well, now what?" Alice asked. "Where do we look for the rest of it?"

"That's a good question," Jason replied. "I'd say look in other music boxes made by the same person."

"Papa Dexter said they are rare, as in museum-piece rare."

Jason winced. "Ouch."

"My goodness," Stella said. "Is it possible that Betsy had other music boxes with hidden compartments?"

"I will check them when I get home," Annie told her, "but I hardly think so. Jason, now that you've played the music, do you have an inkling of who might have written it?"

He shook his head. "As I said, it is similar to Debussy's style, but I've not heard that particular composition." A smile spread across his face. "Wouldn't it be amazing if that bit of music turned out to be an undiscovered score by Debussy?"

Alice gulped audibly.

"Oh, Jason, do you think so?" Annie asked, feeling her eyes go wide.

"No, not really," he said slowly, with considerable regret. "It wouldn't make much sense, would it? Work by a French composer found in a music box in Stony Point, Maine."

"It's possible, though," Alice said. "Anything is possible."

Jason shrugged. "If I were you, I'd not count on it being a Debussy composition. But what I would do, is to get in touch with anyone who might have had any contact with the person who made that music box. They might know something."

"I think that's a good idea, Jason," Annie said.

Stella cleared her throat. "Jason is a very clever man." She tapped the tip of her index finger against her temple. "He has a good brain!"

Jason stood suddenly, as if the three women bestowing smiles on him made him uncomfortable.

"If you don't need me, ma'am, I need to get back to my work."

Stella inclined her head once.

"Goodbye, Jason," Annie said, extending her hand. He shook it and Alice's too.

"Goodbye, ladies. Next time you find an old piece of music, bring it to me." He grinned at them and left the room.

"Well," Annie sighed, "just about the time we have the answer to one thing, two more puzzles pop up. I hope Papa Dexter remembers that carver's family's name."

"Even if he does, Annie, we mustn't forget that the man was an itinerant," Alice said. "His family may be hard to locate. And you know what else?"

"What?"

"How in the world will that family know who composed that bit of music hidden in the music box? I have a feeling this is going to be difficult."

Annie nodded. "I have a feeling you are one hundred percent right."

Back at Grey Gables, Alice went with Annie into the library. They cleared the tops of both desks, and then the two of them gently, but with great eagerness, took each music box from the corner shelf.

They opened each box, and left none of them unexamined. The tops, sides, bottoms, and all corners of every music box received sharp-eyed scrutiny.

"I have pressed every possible tree, heart, flower, and butterfly on every one of these," Annie said, looking at the boxes she had arranged in front of her on Gram's desk.

Alice sighed deeply, gazing at the ones she had put on Charlie Holden's desk. "And I've done the same with these. I've pressed the sides of the smooth ones and poked inside the corners of the ones that open up."

"Let's switch," Annie said. "Maybe one of us missed something."

"All right."

But neither one had missed a thing. The music boxes were empty. The two women looked at each other, disappointed.

"Oh well," Annie said, sighing. "It was worth a shot."

Alice nodded. "But where—oh where—is the rest of that sonata?"

<h1 style="text-align: center;">~ 11 ~</h1>

"Miss Annie, am I doin' it right?" asked a young girl with the greenest eyes Annie had ever seen. She was one of four children sitting in small chairs in a Sunday school room at the Stony Point Community Church. Annie was endeavoring to teach them how to make a crochet chain. All but little, dark-eyed Sean Granger had mastered the chain stitch quite easily. Sean was barely four years old and refused to leave Mattie and Tasha, his older sisters.

Annie looked at the long chain of snug, even stitches the green-eyed girl held out to her.

"You've done a lovely job, Carly," she said. "But try not to hold your yarn so firmly because it makes your stitches too tight. Here, let me show you."

She demonstrated how to control the yarn, and Carly's bright eyes watched every movement, missing nothing.

"OK, Miss Annie. I can do it now."

Annie was amazed how quickly and expertly the child took to crocheting. The other three children in her class at the day camp struggled. At that moment they watched Carly with wide eyes.

"Have you ever done this before?" Annie asked her.

"Nope," Carly said happily, making a chain at the speed of light. She looked up, "But Aunt Freda, she's my grandma's sister, crochets all the time. I like to watch her."

"I see."

"Aunt Freda won't teach me, though, even when I asked and asked and asked. She says she don't have the patience. Sometimes, she tells me I make her too nervous when I watch her, and she makes me go away. Sometimes, she lets me sit down beside her and watch for a long time."

"Miss Annie!" hollered the brown-eyed little boy on her left. "Look, look!"

She turned and saw a tangle of yarn that would take an hour to unknot. She laughed gently, patted his head and said, "Let's get you a new ball of yarn, Sean."

By the time the two hours she had committed to the day camp were over, Annie felt both exhilarated and exhausted. She loved working with the kids, surrounded by their youth and eager voices. It had been too long since she'd been around youngsters, and these children made her long to see her grandchildren. Granted that most of the boys at the day camp were reluctant to learn any needlecraft, and even a few girls balked at the sight of thread, yarn, hooks, and needles. The ones who preferred a less quiet, messier craft went to other rooms where they indulged their creativity with clay or Popsicle sticks or plaster of paris.

She glanced across the hall and into the room directly opposite and saw Alice gathering up her bits and pieces of cross-stitch. She was laughing with three giggling young girls who were telling her knock-knock jokes.

"Will you come back next Friday, Miss Annie?" Carly asked, standing at Annie's elbow. Her eyes shone in expectancy.

Annie smiled down at her. "I surely will. And will you be

here too, Carly?"

Carly dimpled. "Yep! I can't wait to show Aunt Freda what I learned today."

"Me too!" shouted Sean. "My mom will be happy to see the snake I made." He held up the long chain he'd stitched with a lot of assistance from Annie. Tasha and Mattie proudly held up their own chains. Both girls had learned to make the single crochet stitch and had carefully crafted the stitches along the chains.

"And will your sisters return to my class next Friday?" she asked the brown-eyed trio.

"Yes!" they all sang out, then all four kids hugged her so hard, all at the same time, she nearly fell over.

Reverend Wallace called out to Alice and Annie just as they were leaving the church. A portly, gray-haired man with glasses, he was dressed in neatly pressed tan slacks and a simple white shirt.

"Ladies," he said, stretching out his right hand, "thank you so much for spending time today with our children. You can't know what it means to them to have you share your day and your talent."

Annie shook his hand warmly. "It was my pleasure," she said. "I'm away from my daughter and her kids. It's so good to spend time with children."

"Oh, Reverend Wallace," Alice added, "I enjoyed myself so much! I'd forgotten how much fun kids can be."

The minister nodded, smiling. "I'm so glad, Alice. We're so blessed and grateful that both of you showed up to help. We'll see you again next week, then?"

"Oh, yes!" both women chorused.

"Wonderful! Wonderful!" He again shook their hands, beaming.

"That was fun," Alice said as she drove them home in her Mustang. "But I have to admit I'm worn out."

"Me too," Annie said, stretching out the kinks in her back as best she could in the small car. "Would you believe I had temporarily forgotten how noisy and energetic a flock of kids can be?"

"I'm going to go home and take a nap," Alice said, stifling a yawn. "How 'bout you? What are you going to do?"

"Oh, I'm going to put together a picnic lunch for to-morrow."

Annie clamped her lips together, mentally kicking herself when Alice turned her focus from the road ahead to look at her, bright-eyed and curious.

"So, Annie, are you and the honorable mayor going on a picnic?" she asked.

"How'd you know that he's a mayor?" Alice stared at her so long that Annie squawked, "Keep your eyes on the road!"

Alice shifted her attention back and forth between the highway and Annie. "That was a silly question, Annie. Ian Butler has been Stony Point's mayor for several years. You know that."

"Yes, of course. I, uh, I … yes, I know." She felt her face burn.

Alice pulled into the driveway at Grey Gables, braked and turned her full attention on Annie.

"Spill it," she said.

"I beg your pardon?"

"Annie Dawson! We have been friends for too long for

you to keep secrets from me, and I can see as plain as day that you have a secret. So spill it. You know you want to."

Annie blinked. "But I *don't* want to."

"Annie!"

"*Alice!*"

Unfortunately Annie knew her friend well enough to know that she'd worm the information out sooner or later. She sighed.

"I'm going on a picnic with Grady tomorrow."

Alice's eyes got big.

"Grady? You mean Grady Brooks? Grady Brooks from Texas but now from Arkansas? That boy you have refused to talk about even though you had a mad crush on him way, way, way back when?"

Annie pulled in her lips and narrowed her eyes, and then she relaxed her face.

"Yes."

"He's here?"

"Not yet he isn't."

Alice turned ninety degrees in the driver's seat, nearly choking on the shoulder harness of the safety belt to face her friend.

"Annie Dawson, are you telling me he flew all the way from Arkansas up here to Maine just to go on a picnic with you tomorrow? Is that what you're telling me?"

"No, that is not what I'm telling you, Alice MacFarlane. He is in Portland."

"Portland? Really? Why?" Alice's eyes were big as saucers.

"I don't know. He didn't say."

"You finally talked to him?"

"Yes."

Alice took in a deep breath and let it out.

"When did all this come about?"

"He called last night."

"And when were you going to tell me?"

"Actually, Alice, I had not intended to tell you or anyone else."

Alice blinked, and her mouth opened as though she were about to speak. She snapped it shut, narrowed her eyes, and bit her lower lip.

"Keeping it a secret, eh, Annie?" she said finally. "But why? Are you planning to run off and get married or something?"

"Absolutely not! What a thing to say, Alice! And it's just that kind of thinking that made me want to keep our … appointment under wraps. There is no reason that I can see for the whole of Stony Point getting into an uproar, planning a wedding and all sorts of other nonsense. Grady is simply a friend—a childhood friend. Nothing more."

She spoke with such heat and determination that Alice reared back.

"All right, Annie. Excuse me. Sorry I asked." She turned to face forward again and adjusted the shoulder harness away from her throat. "I hope you have a good time." She sat stiffly. Her wounded feelings practically vibrated visibly.

"I apologize if I hurt you, Alice," Annie said, softening her tone. "It's just that … well, I have no intention of replacing Wayne with anyone. Ever."

Alice nodded, relaxing some. "I understand. And truly, I admire your devotion to him." She smiled gently at Annie. "I know how much you loved him."

"Yes, I did. And he loved me." There was a brief silence between them then Annie said, "I need to get busy. Thanks for the ride to the church."

"Any time. Listen, Annie—I hope you have a great time tomorrow. It's always nice to reconnect with old friends. I know it was for me, when you first moved here."

Annie remembered. She returned her friend's smile. "It was, wasn't it?"

"See you later, Annie."

"Bye, now."

Annie hurried up the walkway toward her front door and waved to Alice as the other woman backed out of the driveway.

It really was nice to reconnect. But even better than that was having someone you could count on and spend time with. In spite of the almost-tiff they'd just had, Annie would sooner trade in her right arm than her friendship with Alice. In fact, she almost wished Alice was coming along on the picnic the next day. Having her there would make the whole reunion less awkward.

By early evening, Annie had fried chicken and made potato salad for the next day. She chose a few pieces of fruit to take along and hoped the simple fare would suit Grady Brooks. She seemed to remember his fondness for a crispy drumstick and potato salad with plenty of pickle.

She had just put the food in the refrigerator for the night when her phone rang. She wiped her hands on a nearby dish towel and picked up the handset.

Caller ID displayed the name Alexander Dexter.

"Hello?" Annie said pleasantly into the mouthpiece.

"Mrs. Dawson?"

"Annie, please, Papa Dexter."

"Yes. Annie. How are you?"

"I'm wonderful. And you?"

"The same. Annie, I found that artist magazine that mentioned Malcolm Tyler. He has a great-niece. Her name is Violet Hutchins, and she owns a flower shop in the little town of Ione, Vermont."

— 12 —

The next morning, when she heard the knock on her front door, Annie surprised herself with a feeling of near panic—almost dread. She wanted to stay in the kitchen where she was standing at that moment, safely packing the picnic basket. Then she thought about slipping out the back door and hiding in the woods.

If I don't answer the door, he will go away, she told herself.

After that frantic moment and after inhaling a deep, fortifying breath, Annie firmly tamped down her nerves, smoothed her hair, and walked resolutely to the front door. When she opened it, she saw a face she had never completely forgotten, and she realized why she had lost her young heart to Grady Brooks.

Though three decades had passed since she had last seen him, Grady had changed very little. Of medium height, fine-boned, and handsome, he could play the lead male role in Romeo and Juliet. His curly hair remained dark, though a few silvery strands threaded their way through. Behind stylish frameless glasses, his gray eyes looked back her, clear and bright—and curious.

"Hello, Annie," he said while she stood, feeling like a silly fool. and stared wordlessly at him. He said nothing else, which was so like Grady. He had never been someone to waste breath with needless chatter.

"Grady!" she said, when she gathered her voice and her thoughts. "It's so good to see you again. Won't you please come inside?"

She opened the door, and he stepped through. That moment might have been awkward, but Grady brushed her cheek with a quick kiss, so easy and casual that it might have been given to any friend.

"You look lovely," he said. His slight accent hinted at his Southern roots.

"Thank you, Grady," she said. "You haven't changed at all."

He laughed softly. "It's kind of you to say so."

There was a brief, awkward silence, broken by Annie. "I'm packing our picnic basket," she said. "Would you like a cup of coffee or a glass of tea while I finish?"

He looked surprised. "But, Annie, I had a lunch packed for us in Portland. Did I neglect to tell you that?"

She tried and failed to bite back a laugh. "You never said a word."

He lifted his hands and dropped them in a gesture of defeat. "I think it must have been what's popularly known as a 'senior moment.'"

"Well, come back with me to the kitchen, and I'll put away the food I cooked. We can have it for dinner this evening."

She did not even realize she was going to make this offer until the suggestion spilled from between her lips.

"Great!"

He followed her down the hallway to the sunny yellow and white kitchen. He glanced around, took in the retro appliances, the cabinets with clear glass fronts that showed off Gram's collection of salt and pepper shakers, old dishes, cream pitchers, and other collectibles.

"This makes me think of my grandmother's kitchen," he murmured appreciatively.

"That's the look I was going for!" Annie said with delight. "I've done my best to restore this house to the way I remember it as a child. It's a work in progress and will be for a long time, I imagine. But it's also a work of love."

He nodded. "I can see that." He noticed the fried chicken and potato salad still on the countertop waiting to be stowed into the picnic basket. "Oh, look at what you've done, Annie. You've gone to far too much trouble."

"Not at all," she replied and began stocking the food into the refrigerator. "It won't go to waste."

"This is a grand old house," he said, looking around the kitchen again, tracking the ornate tin ceiling.

"Would you like the tour?" she offered.

"Sure!"

She poured them each a cup of coffee then led him through Grey Gables, pointing out original features and places where repairs had been made.

"This staircase is original, isn't it?" he asked as they ascended to the second floor. "I like how wide it is, and how you've kept the original finish of the wood."

"Oh, I don't think my grandparents would have touched a paintbrush to this lovely old wood, even if they'd been ordered to by law." She laughed. "And neither would I!"

Upstairs, he looked out of each window in all four spacious bedrooms.

"What views!" he exclaimed. "The front lawn and an

ocean view in the master! Annie, you just can't buy something this spectacular."

In the other rooms he nodded appreciatively at the decor Annie maintained, keeping the Victorian era of the home in mind. Downstairs he admired the mahogany tables and chairs in the dining room; he gazed at the wall hangings, gently touched one of Betsy's cross-stitched country scenes.

"Do you do needlework too?" he asked, sipping from his coffee cup.

"I crochet," she explained. "Later, if you want, I'll show you some of my work. Right now, let me take you to my favorite room in Grey Gables—the library."

"I love this room!" he said when they entered the library. "Look at that window seat! And that gorgeous old oak desk!" He gave Annie a wide smile. "These are the kinds of living spaces you see in magazines or in movies, where the homeowner relaxes before the hearth with a good book. I don't have anything like this in my condo."

"You live in a condo? Well, I suppose there really isn't room for a library, is there? In a condo, I mean."

He shook his head, still looking around with a half-smile of pleasure on his face.

"I don't need much room, anyway. My place is pretty small, but it's functional, and it works well for just one person."

Annie paused before she asked, "So I take it you aren't married?"

"No."

The simple reply did not invite further queries, so Annie graciously segued into another topic.

"You see those music boxes in the corner?"

Grady looked at them and nodded.

"Recently there has been an interesting development around here concerning one of Gram's music boxes."

"Oh?"

She invited him to sit in one of the comfy old armchairs, and then as they sipped their coffee, she told him about the rare music box, about Malcolm Tyler's artistry, and about the mysterious, unfinished sonata they had found inside the box on Gram's shelf.

"And you've found nothing to indicate the identity of the composer?"

"Nothing, except the name in the title—'Olivia.' And without a surname, it offers little help. Olivia is not an unusual name, but not that common, either. I don't think I know anyone named Olivia."

"But we're talking about many years ago. I wonder how rare the name was back then?"

"Good point, Grady. And we are talking about someone from a long time ago. Still," she sighed, "it is simply not enough to help us track down the person who wrote the song."

"I find myself wondering if Olivia was a child or an adult," Grady said.

"That's something to consider, isn't it? I suppose ultimately it doesn't matter. However, the song itself is so ... so hauntingly beautiful. Romantic, even. I don't think it was written with a child in mind."

Grady's expression was more curious than ever.

"You've heard the music, then?"

"Oh, yes. Alice and I—Alice is my friend next door—took the score to another friend, and he played it for us.

Oh, it was so lovely." She smiled at the memory, and then her smile faded. "But, it was unfinished. The sonata simply stopped, as if the composer was called away to answer the phone or run an errand, and then never returned."

A frown flickered across Grady's features. "Now that is odd."

"Very odd," she agreed. "I'd love to know what happened to him, if he finished that sonata, why and for whom he wrote it, and if he wrote other pieces."

"I suppose a person could speculate all day about something like this. It is quite a mystery, Annie."

She nodded. "I have run into more puzzles and mysteries than you can imagine since I moved to Stony Point."

"Tell me," he encouraged, so she spent the better part of the next hour telling Grady of the unusual items she had found in the attic and stories behind them. His fascination and curiosity with the subject seemed genuine. It seemed a little peculiar to her how they were able to fall into an easy conversation after so many years, but odder still was how neither one spoke of the past. It was almost as if they were Stony Point friends with no history between them.

"That's amazing," Grady said when she had wrapped up her stories. "And so now, with this music box and the unfinished sonata, do you think you'll continue to pursue looking for the clues and all the odds and ends to the puzzle until you've found all the pieces?"

"I'm certainly going to try." She gazed around the room and sighed. "I tell you, Grady, Gram never threw anything away."

"I believe you," he said, looking around at the walls, the

shelves, and the tabletops. Then he glanced at his watch. "Annie, the day is slipping by. Why don't we leave now, and as we go around looking at the lovely coastal Maine scenery, you can tell me more about this beautiful place you now call home?"

"Sounds like fun to me! Let me go fill some mugs with coffee to take with us."

The time she spent with Grady was fun, but each time conversation lagged, Annie felt pressured to fill the silence. She feared if she didn't, Grady would turn the conversation to days gone by in their shared history, bringing to the broad light of day how she had once felt about him. It would be just too embarrassing.

So she talked. She chattered on about Stony Point, about the Hook and Needle Club, Gram and her treasures. She told him about her daughter and son-in-law, LeeAnn and Herb, and their twins John and Joanna—her only grand-children. She told Grady about her friends, her crocheting project, and the church day camp.

Near the end of the afternoon Annie had exhausted her store of chitchat and she sat, somewhat wilted and pensive, with Grady on a stone bench near Butler's Lighthouse. The pounding rhythm of the surf, the piercing cries of scav-enging gulls, and wind shuffling the sea grasses filled the silence, and she realized with a start—and something like guilt—that Grady had spoken very little. At that moment, he looked nearly as uncomfortable as she felt. She realized she had been rattling like a silly, desperate old woman who spent far too much time by herself. Her face grew hot, and she looked away toward the restless water.

"I'm sorry," she murmured.

"You are? Why?"

She nodded. "I just ..." She raised both hands and let them drop.

"Annie. Look at me."

Reluctantly, she lifted her gaze.

"Are you sorry that you agreed to this? Spending the day with me, I mean?"

"No, of course not." She forced a smile. "It's great seeing you again." More words wouldn't come, and she jumped up, took a few steps, turned around and came back.

"I'm sorry I monopolized the whole day by yammering on like a ... a demented parrot!" she cried, and then she sat down again, face burning in embarrassment.

"Why, Annie, that's all right! Is there something you need to tell me, or perhaps there is something you want to say?"

How in the world could she tell him she had been worried those old feelings from her fourteen-year-old self might return? He had never known she'd once been moony-eyed over him, and to tell him now would be utterly humiliating. At this point she felt more than foolish. She shook her head, wishing she'd never even gotten up that morning. The whole day, except for the tour of Grey Gables, had been one big flop, and she felt she had made a complete fool of herself.

"You might as well tell me," he said with such kindness she almost felt herself ready to confess anyway.

She sighed, started to speak, but then said nothing at all.

"Would you like me to take you home now, and then just go away? I'll do that, if you want me to."

"Oh, Grady," she said, looking up and meeting his eyes.

She felt her face grow even warmer beneath his gaze. How had things got to this point? "I don't even know what to say now."

"How about if you just tell me one thing? Would you tell me why you're so afraid of me?"

She looked at him, surprised and dismayed by the very idea.

"Why, Grady! I'm not afraid of you."

He regarded her without speaking, as if waiting for her to say more. She remembered he used to do that a lot. Say something, and then allow it to marinate within his listener's mind rather than continue to press his point.

"You'd make a good therapist," she told him.

He smiled a little. "Funny you should say that. I'm a licensed clinician."

"You are?"

Well, that made all the sense in the world. And it proved how she had spoiled the day with her mindless, spinning conversation that never once focused on him.

"I am. And that's why I can tell you're afraid, Annie. In fact, you have been afraid all day."

What an outrageous notion! she thought.

She opened her mouth to protest. But slowly, like the trickle of a creek in an early spring thaw Annie realized that, yes, in fact, she was afraid. She was afraid that being with Grady Brooks might awaken something inside her she needed to keep locked away, safe and warm and curled within the confines of her life with Wayne. She feared that silly schoolgirl crush might come back and turn into something stronger and deeper—something much more intense than she ever wanted or needed to feel. She was no longer a romantic fourteen-year-old, but Grady still had those same gray eyes and that same patient expression.

But did she feel that silly quivery feeling the way she did back then? Of course not. Why was she even second guessing herself? Maybe it was because his good looks guaranteed any woman would look at him more than once. Plus, Annie liked and appreciated his quiet, attentive manner; he exuded confidence and caring. Even so, she knew with certainty that she never could care about any man the way she had her husband. Wayne still controlled her heart, and Annie was sure no man could ever replace him.

With her mind no longer battling her sense of right and wrong, and now fully embracing the solid realization that she wanted no man to step into Wayne's shoes, Annie found she could finally relax. At long last, the nagging need to distract herself and Grady from any conversation that touched on their personal lives finally began to ebb, bit by bit.

"I guess you're right. I am a little afraid," she said, finally. She gave him a small, apologetic smile. "But I'm not afraid of you. I mean, I'm not afraid you're going to hit me on the head and drag me off somewhere."

"But can you tell me what it is you fear?"

She could, but did she want to? What purpose would it serve for her to bring up those silly old feelings of which Grady knew nothing.

"I'm just being foolish, Grady. Let's forget it, shall we?" she said, putting as much enthusiasm in her voice as possible. She even gave him a bright smile as she started gathering up the scraps of their picnic.

He studied her face a few more moments, and then

nodded. "OK, Annie."

"So you're a therapist," she said, after a short silence. "Does that get in the way of being a mayor?"

He chuckled as he folded the cloth that they had spread across the picnic table.

"Cooper City, population three thousand and forty-two, is a pretty little town in the heart of the Ozark Mountains. There is not a whole lot of municipal government for me to take care of. In fact, it seems to me that the position of mayor is more of a title than anything else. And there is no salary!" He chuckled a little bit. "The police chief is also the pastor of the church, and the city council is made up of our mortician, the owner of the convenience store, the wife of a rancher, the dentist and me."

"That's an eclectic mix."

He nodded. "It is. But we all get along, and we keep the town up and running."

"That's great, Grady. I'd hate to pick up the paper some-day and read that a small war had broken out among the councilmen of Cooper City, Arkansas."

They laughed together, and Annie was so glad the tension had finally broken.

"You said you're friends with the local mayor?" he asked.

"Yes. For Ian it's a full-time job. I think he really enjoys it."

"Stony Point is larger than Cooper City. I'm sure he's busier taking care of the town than I am."

Annie agreed as they walked toward his car, and then she asked him, "When you do plan to return to Arkansas?"

"I'm not sure yet. This is the first vacation I've had in a long time. An old college chum lives in Portland, so I came up here to visit. We hadn't seen each other in years."

"How nice!" she said as he opened the trunk to stow the picnic basket and cloth. "Reliving old times can be such fun." She stopped abruptly. She and Grady had not relived old times at all. But glancing at him, she saw he kept no account of what she felt to be her failure that day. A big smile wreathed his face.

"The visit is going well, and if things continue as they have been, I may stay a while longer."

This seemed to Annie a rather curious statement. She waited for him to say more, but he didn't. Instead, he closed the trunk, and then opened the passenger door for her.

"You always were a gentleman, Grady," she told him as she got in, remembering Wayne opening the passenger door for her from time to time when he was feeling especially genteel. They had always joked about his gallantry when he did that.

"That's me. A gentleman to the very core."

As they drove back toward Grey Gables, he said, "Annie, it has been so good to see you again. When we hung around together as kids, you always could make me smile. You'd spin such accounts of your family's ventures as missionaries, or tell me about the summers with your grandmother up here in Maine. Talking with you was always so easy, and somehow, after we had spent an hour or two visiting, some of the clutter and questions in my mind were swept away, even if we never talked about what was bothering me."

"Really?" she said, totally surprised by his words. "I thought I was more of a hanger-on than anything else."

"Of course not, Annie. You were young, but you were

smart, and you were a good listener."

"So were you, Grady." She laughed a little. "If we were both such good listeners, which one of us did the talking?"

He smiled. "I never thought of that."

He fell silent, and for the first time, Annie sensed disquiet in him. He shifted a little uncomfortably in the driver's seat, checked the rearview mirror, and glanced at his gas gauge. He ran his fingers through his hair.

"Grady? Is something wrong?"

"I have to apologize!" he burst out.

She blinked. "You do? To whom?"

"To you."

"Me? Why?"

"A month or so ago, I was surfing the Internet, just relaxing for a while, and decided to do some online searches for old friends. You know, typing in a name and seeing what came up—Jim Tennison is a doctor in Colorado Springs, Frannie Hardcastle has an eBay business; then there's my friend Chris who is in Portland, and so on and so forth. I'd made a trip back to the old neighborhood several years ago, heard that you'd married someone named Dawson, so I typed in your name. I found several women with the name Annie Dawson, but when I discovered that one of them lived in Stony Point, Maine, I recalled you talking about visiting your grandmother here."

He hesitated, and then continued. "Something has been gnawing on my mind for a little while, giving me no peace. When I decided to make this trip to Maine, I realized that I really needed the calming presence of my old friend Annie Spencer, because you were always so clear-headed and wise.

So I called you. Then I chickened out and hung up. Then I called you again, and you know the rest."

She gaped at him. "Are you saying that you got in touch because you needed me?"

"Yes! And I apologize, Annie."

"Why are you apologizing? I think it's great that you thought so highly of me that you believe I could be of help."

"I should have been more open with you right from the first, of course. I just didn't want you to feel obligated … you know, because we knew each other when we were kids."

"For goodness sake!" she said faintly. Here all this time she'd been thinking he wanted to have a romance with her, and instead he'd needed her in a way she could not fathom.

"Grady," she said, leaning toward him, "I'll be more than happy to help you in any way I can. Please tell me what you need me to do."

"You've already done it," he said, smiling at her.

She leaned back. "I have? What did I do? And when did I do it? I've done nothing but rattle on like a magpie all day!"

"But you have proven to me that life flows, that bits and pieces make up our days, and that hesitating is the greatest way to miss out on enjoying life. A person needs to take leaps of faith sometimes."

She studied his profile, but her confusion remained. "I'm afraid I don't understand."

He glanced at her and then back at the road. "You uprooted yourself from the only life you'd known for many years, and you made a new life for yourself up here. You've not been living in Stony Point that long, but look at you, Annie, up to your neck in friends and activities."

"It came at a cost, though. I left behind family and friends in Texas."

"I realize that. There is never gain without some loss. But you picked up and started over, and it's good now. Isn't it?"

"Yes. It's good. It's very good, and I still maintain contact with family and folks back in Texas." She cocked her head to one side. "Grady, what aren't you telling me? What's all this about?"

He shook his head. "I'm not ready to say, but I promise to tell you later."

"Grady Brooks! After everything you just said, you're going to leave me hanging—curious and confused?"

"Afraid so." He grinned at her and reached out and squeezed her hand briefly. "But only for now."

"Hmm."

She narrowed her eyes at him. He laughed quietly, but he said nothing more about whatever was on his mind.

When they were nearly to Grey Gables, she said, "Grady, if you're still in Portland next Saturday, I'd love for you to come to a cookout I'm going to have. We're going to have burgers and all the usual things that go with them."

He considered the invitation, and then replied, "Sounds like fun, and I'd like to come. Would it be all right with you if I bring my friend?"

"Sure!" she said. "I'm inviting virtually all of Stony Point—well, all the ones I know, anyway, so as far as I'm concerned, the more the merrier. Besides the barbecue, there will be baked goods available for purchase, Princessa jewelry, and Divine Décor items for the home. Plus, you can meet all my wonderful friends I've been talking about."

"Annie," he said with a big smile, "if I'm still here in a week, I will definitely come to the cookout."

"With your friend."

"Absolutely!"

Grady dropped Annie off at Grey Gables, but he declined an invitation to come inside and eat the food she had prepared earlier.

"It's getting late, and I need to get back to Portland, but thanks for the offer, Annie. You're great."

They gave each other a brief, friendly hug before parting company.

She got out of the car, but just before she closed the door, he said, "I hope you find out who wrote that music, Annie. It's an interesting little mystery."

"All mysteries are interesting, if you know what I mean." She gave him a significant look, but he simply grinned at her. "I'll let you know what I learn."

"Great!"

"And you'd better let me know what all your cryptic talk was about," she warned him with a smile. "You don't want me to stay awake all night wondering about it, do you?"

"Don't lose any sleep. I'll fill you in later," he said. Lifting one hand in a wave, he added, "See you later, Annie."

"Bye-bye, Grady," she said and closed the door. She watched as he drove away, and then went into the house feeling much better—even if more mystified—than she had in the last few days.

~ 13 ~

On Monday morning, after Annie finished her breakfast and fed Boots, she picked up the telephone and dialed the number she had written down for the Bright Petals Flower Shop in Ione, Vermont. A pleasant female voice greeted her.

"Good morning," Annie said. "My name is Annie Dawson, and I'm calling for Violet Hutchins."

"This is Violet. May I help you?"

Annie explained the purpose of the call while the other woman periodically enthusiastically inserted, "Yes, I see!" and "Oh, my!" and "How interesting!"

Finally she said, "I'm assuming you need information from me about Malcolm Tyler?"

"Yes," Annie agreed, "and I'd love to know who wrote that music we found hidden inside the box."

"Ooo! I don't blame you! Maybe that piece of music was written by some famous composer."

"That's a slim possibility," Annie said, "but I'm keeping an open mind. Ms. Hutchins, I know it's a long shot, but I'm wondering if you might know to whom Malcolm Tyler sold his music boxes. If I can find out who used to own that music box, maybe I can track down the composer."

"You know, I think I can help you!" Violet said with such enthusiasm the phone nearly glowed. "It might take me a few days, but I know that my great-uncle kept a log of everyone he carved anything for."

"That seems rather odd to me," Annie said. "What I mean is that, from what little I've learned, he was rather ... um ..." She paused, seeking the right word.

"I think I know what you mean! It's always seemed strange that he would do something so mundane and businesslike as keeping a list of his customers when he was so careless in other aspects of his life. But he was such a free spirit, so I suppose that means he didn't feel bound by convention."

"Would you please tell me what you know about him?"

Violet laughed lightly. "I don't know very much. The family rarely mentioned him. I do know that he traveled all the time, but even then, he kept to himself. I wonder—can you be a hermit and an itinerant at the same time?"

"Good point," Annie said. "I'd never thought about that. Maybe 'hermit' isn't the right word, though. 'Eccentric' might be the better term."

"Yes! I think you're right. Malcolm hardly left any imprint of himself on anything other than his unique carving and wood-crafting style."

"Since he was so artistic, is it possible your uncle might have written the music we found inside the box?"

Violet laughed. "I suppose it's possible, but I don't know. Truly, none of us in the family know much about him. Not to be callous, Mrs. Dawson, but I'm not so sure any of us has ever cared very much. He was such a black sheep— such an embarrassment to many of the relatives. But not so much to me, of course. I don't embarrass easily. These days, we've all been so busy with our own lives, you know, and old family history seems like such a waste of time. That said, I think I might be able to help you a little. I just might know where those records are."

"That would be wonderful if you do," Annie said, though she felt a deep pang for anyone whose legacy was ignored by their own blood.

"Tell me what the music box looks like. That's how he logged them into his ledger."

"I think the wood is chestnut, but I'm not sure. The carving is quite intricate, with lots of ivy, and there's a heart on top with lovebirds in the center."

"My, that sounds like a lot of work just for a music box!" Violet exclaimed. "Well, Mrs. Dawson, I won't promise you anything, but let me do a little inquiry. If you'll give me your phone number, I'll call you when and if I find something."

"Thank you so much. I look forward to hearing from you again."

After she hung up the phone, Annie flopped into her favorite chair and sprawled like a rag doll. To think she might actually learn the identity of the composer of that lovely piece of music warmed her heart. And wouldn't it be nice if she also could find out about Olivia?

Boots jumped up into her lap.

"Hey there, kitty," Annie said, tickling the cat under her soft, pointed chin. "Life is full of mystery, isn't it?" She looked into the cat's green eyes. "I wish you could tell me who Malcolm carved that music box for. Did that person write the music? Who was Olivia, and what does she have to do with anything? Was she even real?" Boots closed her eyes, stretched her neck, and purred with joy. "And here's another quandary," Annie told the contented cat. "What's going on with Grady Brooks? What in the world did I say to him that caused him to make some momentous decision? And what was he deciding about?"

She stopped rubbing the cat and stared at nothing on the opposite wall. Boots nudged her head against Annie's fingers.

When the telephone rang, its sudden sound startled Annie so much that she jumped and sat straight up. Boots, affronted by the gesture, leaped off her lap and strolled away, completely indignant.

"Annie!" boomed a friendly voice she recognized the moment she answered the telephone.

"Papa Dexter. How are you?"

"I'm doing well, Annie, and I have good news for you."

She sat up even straighter.

"It has long been my opinion," she said, "that good news is always a good thing."

"I've often subscribed to that notion myself," he said with a chuckle.

"I have a bit of good news too, but tell me yours first," Annie said.

"All right. My good news is I fixed your music box."

"Really? You mean it plays now?"

"Like brand-new. The comb that strikes the notes was missing, and the key was simply jammed. I unjammed the key and replaced the comb from an old broken music box I had here."

"Papa Dexter, that is good news! I am thrilled beyond words," she said. "I can't wait to hear it!"

"Would you like to come out and pick it up?"

"Absolutely! May I come now?"

"You certainly may. In fact, I'll put the coffee on and be waiting for you. And when you get here, share with me your good news."

Annie ran upstairs and slipped into a pair of khaki slacks and a sleeveless pale yellow blouse. She slid her feet into a pair of sandals, ran a brush through her hair, grabbed her purse and dashed downstairs.

"See you later, Boots," she called to the cat, who was stoically sitting in the middle of the hallway blinking at her.

When Annie got to Papa Dexter's door, the elderly man greeted her as warmly as an old friend.

"Didn't you bring Alice with you?" he said, peering over her shoulder.

Annie bit her lower lip for a second and fought a tiny pang of guilt.

"I was so excited that you fixed the music box I didn't even think to ask her."

His blue eyes twinkled. "I think she'll forgive you. Come in, my dear. The coffee is waiting … and so is the music box."

Inside his cozy home, he led her to the small dining table where he'd set out cups, small plates, and slices of yellow poppy seed pound cake.

"Please sit, Annie. I'll pour coffee, and you help yourself to the cake. It's rather good."

She savored the first, lemony bite. "Did Alice MacFarlane make this?"

He laughed. "No. I did." He filled her cup, and then met her eyes. "A man who lives alone for many years can become a good cook, if he's of a mind to do so."

He left the room, but returned a few moments later with the music box.

"I know you didn't come to Dexter Cove to merely sit and have cake. Here it is."

She dabbed her lips and fingertips with a paper napkin, and then leaned forward as the old man showed her what he had done.

"It was just a matter of finding the right part and having the right tools," he said. "And luckily an old clutterbug like me has an abundance of parts and tools."

"May I hear it?" she said, breathlessly, coffee and cake forgotten.

"Of course! We'll just wind it up and play it."

He gave the key a few deft twists and the delicate sound filled the room. Annie had heard the song only once before, but she immediately recognized the unfinished sonata for Olivia that Jason had played from the composition found in the music box.

"My goodness," she whispered, leaning forward even further, watching the teeth of the little metal comb strike each tiny note.

Papa looked up, silvery eyebrows raised in silent a question.

"Papa," she said, her eyes wide, "that is the music that was on the manuscript we found inside the box."

His mouth dropped open and he too, stared at the small movement winding down.

"Are you sure?" he asked when the music fell silent.

"Positively. Of course, it's only a portion, but still …"

The pair gazed at the music box, as if expecting something even more unexpected would reveal itself. Finally they looked up and met each other's eyes.

"Extraordinary," he breathed.

Annie nodded. "Very much so!" After another silent, stunned moment, she asked, "Papa Dexter, do you think Malcolm Tyler made the movements that went inside the boxes he carved?" she asked.

He sat back and exhaled deeply, as if he'd been holding his breath for a long time.

"I don't know, Annie. It's possible. I had always assumed he bought them from a maker somewhere, but maybe he did make them."

"If that were the case, then don't you think he was the one who wrote the music?"

He stroked his beard and gazed down at the music box again.

"That's very likely," he said at last, "but I don't know. There just isn't much known about the man."

"His great-niece said he pretty much kept to himself."

He looked up. "You've talked to her, have you?"

"Yes. I talked with her this morning just before you called, actually. And that was my good news for you."

"Please share."

"It seems the family doesn't know a lot about the man," she said. "Apparently his artistic bent was a source of embarrassment."

"Unfortunately, that happens all too often to artists born to more 'earthbound' families. The artists, musicians, and writers see the world through eyes different from the rest of us. A color, a spot of sunlight, a slight sound, a random phrase—all these things can spark something new within their minds, and they set about recreating it so the rest of us can share the vision."

She pondered his words.

"Gram was like that. Her needlepoint was so unique that no one else has ever been able to duplicate it. The fact that she was able to envision the stitches, the colors, and the images before any of it existed simply boggles my mind. Or take Kate Stevens. She works at A Stitch in Time in town. She can create the most amazing crocheted items you've ever seen!"

He smiled.

"You have an appreciation for art."

"I do," she sighed, "and not a lot of talent for it, I'm sorry to say. I love to crochet, but I must follow a pattern. I make lovely things that way, but to create something that hasn't been there before ..." She shook her head. "I don't have that ability."

He reached over, and patted her hand. "There's something to be said for following patterns too, my dear."

She smiled at him. "You're right, Papa. You are exactly right."

He refilled her coffee cup, and then said, thoughtfully, "Something else puzzles me about this music box."

"Oh?" She sipped her coffee. "What's that?"

"That comb was deliberately broken."

Annie frowned and set down the cup.

"How do you know that? Couldn't it have just been damaged by someone playing the music too often, or winding the key too tightly, or even dropping it?"

He shook his head.

"I don't believe so, no. Look here." He pointed to the repaired part. "The comb is screwed in so it couldn't just fall out. Besides that, the teeth were actually broken from the original piece. Look."

He took the little bit of metal from his shirt pocket. "See? The teeth have been sheered away. The destruction had to be deliberate."

Annie's frown deepened.

"Why would anyone do that?" she asked.

"That's a good question," Papa Dexter said. "And why would anyone hide a music manuscript inside a box that was quite a trick to get open?"

"Good point. And it is even more curious that the sonata inside was the same tune that the music box played."

They were silent for a time, sightlessly staring at each other, thinking their own thoughts about this newest twist on what continued to be a growing mystery.

"Well," Annie said after a bit, "I hope Violet Hutchins can tell me something, but to be frank, she really didn't sound all that interested in the man."

"That's too bad." He fastened the two parts of the music box together and lifted it. "All you have to do is look at this and take note of how it was crafted to know that Malcolm Tyler was a genius." He ran his hand over the carved flowers and the tiny birds—and then met Annie's eyes. "You let me know what you find out, will you?"

"I will."

She watched the old man continue to study the box, caressing it with his fingertips. He was such a dear person with such a unique personality, and she was grateful she had been granted the opportunity to meet him. Papa Dexter was someone she'd like to spend more time with and get to know better.

"Papa," she said, and he glanced up. "Are you busy Saturday?"

He shook his head, giving her a smile. "These days I'm never very busy. Why?"

"I'm having a barbecue at Grey Gables—an old-fashioned, down-home Texas cookout—and I'm inviting everyone I can think of. I'd love for you to come."

A smile creased his face and shone deep in his eyes.

"Why, thank you! I'd like that. I don't believe I've ever been to an old-fashioned, down-home Texas cookout."

"Well, it won't be exactly like the ones we used to have back home, but it'll be fun. Folks are bringing food, so it has turned into a potluck barbecue. There will be things for you to buy, if you're interested—Princessa jewelry and Divine Décor, and some of Alice MacFarlane's delicious baked goods."

"It sounds like a good time. In fact, it sounds like a real ripsnorter." He chuckled. "You familiar with that term, ripsnorter?"

"I've heard it. I think it means an extra-good time."

"You're right. An excellent time, in fact. Say, uh, Annie, do you think ... is there a possibility that Stella will be there?"

"Stella Brickson?"

He nodded, looking a little embarrassed.

Annie smiled. "She said she would be."

He beamed. "Then you can count on me showing up!"

~ 14 ~

After Annie left Papa Dexter's with the restored music box encased in bubble wrap and tucked safely on the passenger's side floor of the Malibu, she stopped by the grocery store for several items. Instead of going straight home to Grey Gables after shopping, she went to Alice's.

"Annie!" Alice said, smiling big as she opened the door. "Come inside, I want to show you what I'm doing."

With the grocery bags in her arms, Annie followed her friend to the kitchen. She stopped abruptly in the doorway and gawked at the scene. She had never seen so many pans and baking sheets in one kitchen in all her life.

Alice laughed at Annie's stunned expression.

"I call it controlled chaos. I had to borrow from everyone I knew. If I'm going to sell baked goods, I need to have a plan to get it all done. Over there will be my breads." She pointed to loaf and muffin pans on one countertop. "There will be cookies, where those cookie sheets are." She tapped a tower of round cake pans. "And here is where my cakes will be put together. You weren't home, or I would have been at your door, borrowing." She eyed the sacks Annie held. "What's that?"

Annie looked down at her burden, and then glanced around for an empty space to put down the groceries. She settled for a spot on the small dining table.

"This is flour, sugar, baking powder, that sort of thing."

"Why, Annie!"

"This bake sale was my idea, and don't tell me you don't need this stuff."

"I need them, of course, and I'll use them. Thank you! But, really, you—"

"I expect to keep half of any unsold baked goods. I doubt there will be any, but if so, I want half of them. If there are none left, then you must make me a loaf of bread, a batch of cookies, and a pie."

Alice laughed and gave her a quick hug. "You got it! Thanks for being such a good friend, Annie."

Annie glanced around again.

"You certainly have your work cut out for you. Is there anything I can do to help?"

Alice's expression clearly conveyed gratitude.

"I don't think so, but thank you for offering," she said. "I believe I have it all under control. I have my work areas organized, my baking times scheduled, plenty of ingredients, and all the utensils I need." She smiled. "I guess the best thing for you to do is leave me to it."

"Are you throwing me out?"

Alice linked her arm with Annie's at the elbow and escorted her regally to the front door.

"In a manner of speaking, yes."

"Hmm. Then maybe you don't want to hear the latest about the music box?"

Alice gave her a look of mock outrage.

"Where did you come up with such a misplaced notion as that? When do I ever not want to know the latest about anything, especially the mystery about the music box?"

"Come to think of it," Annie said, "never. The latest is this: Papa Dexter fixed it!"

"He fixed it? You mean it plays now?"

"That is exactly what I mean."

Alice clapped her hands. "Oh, I want to hear it!"

"I'll bring it to the Hook and Needle Club meeting tomorrow." She took a step out the front door, paused and looked over her shoulder at her friend, and added, "You are far too busy to hear it now."

"Annie Dawson! I want to hear it now."

"See you tomorrow," she called as she reached her car. She gave the indignant Alice a friendly little wave, along with an impudent little smile, and got in the Malibu.

Sometimes, she thought, still smiling, *the longer you wait for something, the more fun it is.*

Besides, Alice really did have a lot to do, and showing her the music box right then would doubtless lead to an hour or two of speculation and conversation, not to mention chitchat and casual gossip.

Annie found a message on her answering machine when she got home.

"Hello. This is Violet Hutchins at the Bright Petals Flower Shop. I have the information you requested. Please call me."

"My goodness, that was fast," Annie told the machine.

She had not expected to hear from Violet for days, if not weeks, especially as the woman seemed to have little interest in her great-uncle or anything about him.

She pushed the numbers to return the call and again

was greeted with cheer and enthusiasm.

"I'm so glad I'm able to help you," Violet told Annie. "My daughter absolutely loves all that dusty old family history and has collected what little the Tyler family saved. At lunch, when I mentioned to her what you were looking for, she said, 'Why Mom, I have that book with all the other family papers!'" Violet laughed. "I don't know where that young woman gets her fascination with the dead and gone, but lucky for you, she has it." She laughed again.

Annie heard the flippant words, but could hardly take them in. What would happen to memories, to the passed-down craftsmanship, and to the pride of heritage if everyone felt the way Violet Hutchins did? What if Annie cared nothing about Betsy Holden's beautiful legacy to the world? How many people had been touched, not only by her work, but also by her kindness and care?

Thank goodness that her daughter, as busy as she was with all the duties life demanded of her, still had the time and interest to care about who and what had gone through the world before her. Annie shuddered even to think that her own grandmother's legacy would be left to drift into anonymity, or worse, completely forgotten.

"Well, I do appreciate your speedy response," she told Violet as pleasantly as possible. "What did your daughter find?"

"I have it right here."

Annie heard the shuffling of paper, and then Violet said, "Malcolm was very good to record details of every music box made, when he made it, and for whom. The man who ordered a music box carved with ivy, lovebirds, and a heart on top was Peter Starne." She spelled it for Annie.

"The order was given on June 8, 1939, and completed on November 30, 1939."

Gratefully, Annie carefully wrote down every word and every number. She had another question, and knew it was a long shot.

She asked, "Do you know if Malcolm made the movements that went inside the box?"

"Oh, my," Violet replied, laughing lightly. "I have no idea." Annie heard the shuffle of paper, and after a few moments, Violet continued, "I see nothing about it in his book. It seems logical, doesn't it, that as meticulous as his record keeping is about the wooden boxes, he'd be just as detailed if he made the movements. I'd say he probably did not make them. Don't you agree?"

"I think that, more than likely, you are right."

It stood to reason, then, that the music-box movements were made elsewhere. And if that were the case, whoever wrote the unfinished sonata was someone who either could build movements or had commissioned the musical piece to be built. Nothing, though, explained why the music had been hidden, or why the comb had been broken so the music could not be played.

"Thank you for all your help, Violet," she said. "If you come across any information that you think might help me, would you please get in touch?"

"Oh, I surely will!" Violet said merrily. "I'll tell my daughter this evening to go through her box and see if she can find out anything else about Malcolm."

"I appreciate your help."

After Annie hung up the phone, she stood a moment

staring down at it, contemplating family—her parents, her daughter, her grandmother, and her aunt. Although she had not always been with her mother and father during their mission trips, she loved them deeply and never doubted for a moment that they loved and cared for her. From her Aunt Susan she had received much warmth and guidance. Her grandmother could not have been more doting and wise, and Betsy had passed down a legacy that had molded Annie's life—not to mention a treasure trove of beautiful memories.

It went without saying that Annie likewise treasured the close relationship she had with her daughter. She admitted that there were times when LeeAnn's busy life seemed to leave Annie on the periphery, but Annie knew the strong cord between them could never be severed, neither by distance nor by busy days. Although Maine and Texas were hundreds of miles apart, she felt LeeAnn's spirit with her always, and she knew in the deepest part of her heart that her daughter felt the same.

A surge of homesickness and longing overtook Annie, nearly swallowing her with its unexpected arrival. She'd been in Stony Point long enough that waves of homesickness were fewer and further between, but still, once in a while, the urge to see her loved ones seized her tightly and did not let go easily. If she could not embrace her daughter right then, at least she could hear her voice. She picked up the telephone and dialed.

"Honey, it's Mom," she said when LeeAnn answered. "How are you?"

"Hi, Mom! This is weird because I was just this minute thinking about you."

"Were you? That's a lovely thing to know, honey."

"Yes. I was thinking how you were always so calm and level-headed in times of upheaval. Mom, you have no idea how I wish I could be more like that!"

LeeAnn's tone, fringed with an almost frantic tone, caused Annie concern.

"Is something wrong, honey?"

"Oh, not really," she sighed. "Just the usual madhouse around here, too much to do and not enough time to get it all done. That's not going to change anytime soon." She laughed a little, and then hurried to add, "Not that I want it to, of course, but sometimes a break would be nice."

"Well, I'm sorry you're having such a hectic time. Should I call back later?"

"Oh, no! Please—I always want to talk to you, no matter how wild it gets around here. But the bad news is that the twins seem to have caught some kind of virus, and they are both sick."

"Oh, dear! I hope it isn't serious. Have you taken them to the doctor?"

"Actually, I think it's just a little bug that has been going around at church. They're in bed, and I'm keeping a close eye on them. They aren't that sick. I mean, they keep begging me to let them get up and play. But since they're running a slight fever, I think they need to stay in bed a day or two."

"I'm sure they'll be back to normal soon, then," Annie said. "You're a good mom, LeeAnn. I won't keep you. I just wanted to call and say hi and to hear your voice. Are you and Herb all right? You haven't got the bug too, have you?"

"No, we're fine. Is everything all right with you, Mom?"

"Everything is fine," Annie said stoutly, "but I just had a rather disturbing conversation with someone."

"Tell me about it. The kids are quiet right now, and I could go for a little break."

Annie recounted her exchange with Violet. "I just found the whole thing so disquieting," she concluded, "maybe more than I should have. Actually, I feel sorry for their family because, except for the daughter, they have missed so much. Imagine having someone like Malcolm Tyler in your family, but not caring about him. Apparently they had little to do with him when he was alive, and certainly no one but the one daughter cares now. I find it so sad."

"I understand, Mom. I feel the same way. And you're right. It is sad."

"In case I haven't told you lately, honey, I'm so grateful that you're my child. And I'm just so happy I can share Gram's legacy with you and know it's something you won't throw away or disregard. I hope you teach the twins how important family is, even those family members who've passed on."

"Of course I will, Mom! In fact, I do. Just the other night we were looking at the photo album and those pictures of me when I was really young. They couldn't believe I'd once been their age!"

It felt good to laugh with her daughter.

"Then I showed them photos of Gram; they asked me all kinds of questions about her. Joanna said, 'I want to make pictures with a needle and thread like Grandma Betsy.'"

"I am so glad to hear that!" Annie said. "I hope you encourage her, LeeAnn. As long as we pass down what we've learned, these old arts will never be left behind and forgotten."

"You can count on it, Mom. Not so sure John cares, but Herb is going to make sure he learns some kind of craft like that. Herb firmly believes everyone should be able to make something with their hands. He says it's good for the soul."

"And I agree," Annie declared.

"I was sure you would. Don't you worry. We will honor Gram—and you. We love you, Mom." She paused and Annie heard the sound of a child in the background. "Mom, I'm sorry, but Joanna is calling for me. It's just a matter of time before John does the same. Oh! There he goes. He's calling now. I have to go."

"Yes, you go take care of those sweet kids. Give them a kiss from their grandmother. I love you, honey."

"Love you too. Bye now."

Annie clicked the phone off as tears graced her cheeks.

~ 15 ~

Annie was the last member of the Hook and Needle Club to show up the next day. Along with her crocheting project and the carefully wrapped music box, she toted a huge cache of excitement into A Stitch in Time. She knew the women would be as intrigued as she was when she played the music for them and told them about the manuscript she'd discovered inside.

Of course, if Annie thought her discovery would be fresh news to the women who made up the Hook and Needle Club, she needed to adjust her thinking. Word had gotten around about the hidden musical score, and her crafting friends greeted her with unrestrained enthusiasm the moment she walked in.

"You brought it, didn't you, Annie?" Peggy called from where she sat, busily working on her wall hanging.

Annie's eyes sparkled as she looked at her friends. "Indeed I did. And did you—"

"Excuse me, ladies, for interrupting," Mary Beth said. "Annie, you know we are all dying to see the music box and hear it play, but it seems best if we take care of business first."

It took a moment for the whispered speculations to fall silent as the women reluctantly and momentarily subdued their interest to focus on their projects and on Mary Beth, who stood before them to speak.

"First," Mary Beth said, adjusting her glasses just a bit as she looked at the women in their various stages of crafting, "let's discuss how it went at the day camp last week. Reverend Wallace called this morning and said he was so pleased with what you ladies did."

"I was there Wednesday afternoon," Peggy said, peering critically at her stitches on the wrong side of the piece. She glanced up. "I wasn't sure I could get off work, but when I explained what we were doing, the boss said it was all right for me go, as long as I was back in time for the dinner crowd. It was great fun. I'm teaching two twelve-year-olds, and they seem to be learning how to put together a nine-patch square very quickly."

"I'm having such fun at the day camp!" Kate put in. "There's a boy, Henry Salisbury—spelled like the steak—and he was especially intrigued by crochet patternmaking. He's a math whiz and a star soccer player, and would you believe he's just as proficient with a hook and yarn? I think it's just so fabulous that a boy wants to learn. It's about time fellows realize that needlework isn't sissy."

"Oh, I believe it's becoming more accepted all the time," Mary Beth said. "Who knows? One day we might have a guy in our Hook and Needle Club."

"That would be fun!" Alice said, laughing.

"Well, thank goodness, I got the easy job," Stella piped up, putting a halt to the speculation of male Hook and Needle Club members before it went further. "I'm teaching three older girls who want to knit those long scarves that are so popular right now."

Gwen laughed softly as she finished knitting a dishcloth.

"Only you would think that was easy, Stella. You're so good at it."

"And what about you, Gwen?" Annie asked. "How'd it go for you?"

"I'm afraid I'm simply teaching knitting basics to some young girls. They certainly complained a lot. Maybe I'm not such a good teacher." She glanced at Stella. "Maybe I should send them to your class."

Stella frowned at her, and Gwen shrugged. "I guess that's a no."

"That most definitely is a no," Stella said.

"Well, I think Annie and I had a great time," said Alice. "At least I did! I believe I had more fun teaching the kids how to cross-stitch than they did learning. We laughed and sang the whole time."

"That's true," Annie agreed, laughing. "I almost came across the hall and took your class because y'all were having such a good time. But I had a great group of new crocheters— young and eager. It's great to pass on what I've been taught."

"Well, I just think it's wonderful, working with kids," Alice said. "I hope we do this again."

"Oh, so do I," Annie said just as the door opened, and Jenny Simon from the Nocturnal Loons band walked in.

Jenny greeted the others with a wave and a warm smile, but she said, "Annie, I need to talk to you."

Uh oh, Annie thought as she walked away from the group with Jenny.

"Annie, I am so sorry, but the band is not going to be able to make it Saturday. There has been a death in Rory and Billy's family—their paternal grandfather in Augusta."

"Oh, I'm so sorry to hear that! Please convey my condolences."

Jenny smiled gently, sadly. "Yes, I will, thank you. The
guys were very close to their grandfather, so the next few
weeks are going to be hard on them."

Annie placed her hand on Jenny's arm. "It's so hard to
lose someone you love."

The other woman nodded. "Yes, it is. I'm really sorry
that we can't make it Saturday, but I do thank you, Annie,
for being so understanding."

After Jenny left, Annie rejoined the group, feeling much
less cheery than she had a few moments earlier. The death of
the men's grandfather had served to remind her of losing Betsy, and of not having the opportunity to tell her grandmother
goodbye. She regained her seat, picked up her crocheting
and silently began to stitch, lost for a moment in recollec-
tion. When she realized the other women were quieter than
usual, she looked up to see most of them were gazing at her.

"Are you all right?" Mary Beth asked softly.

"Yes, I'm fine, but do you know Jenny?"

Every woman seemed to know the girl.

"She's in the band with Rory and Billy Flynn that I had
scheduled for the party this weekend. Their grandfather just
passed away."

"Oh no!" Gwen gasped, putting down her newest dishcloth, this one a dark green. "I'm so sorry to hear that. He
used to live here, years ago. He was a dear old fellow."

"Yes, he was," Mary Beth agreed, and for a few minutes
the women who had known the man shared their memories.

"I remember when I was girl," Kate said, "and he brought

two bushel baskets of apples to our church for everyone to share. They were the best, juiciest apples ever."

"John told me about the time Mr. Flynn came into the bank and paid all the arrearages on a certain person's mortgage. He never told me who, but wasn't that a wonderful gesture on Mr. Flynn's part?"

"I'm sorry I never got a chance to meet him," Annie murmured.

Silence settled over the group for a while as the ones who knew the elderly man each gave tribute to him in their own thoughts.

After a while, Kate cleared her throat and asked, "Annie, does this mean you'll not have live music at the cookout?"

Annie looked up.

"Yes, I suppose it does. Unless someone here knows of another local small band who would perform on short notice?"

"I don't know of any. Stony Point is pretty limited," Kate said.

"I don't know anyone, either," Mary Beth said, and the others shook their heads. "You might have to use a CD player, if you want music."

In the chair beside Annie's, Alice twitched. That was a good signal that she had something to say. Annie glanced at her friend as Alice put down her hook, yarn, and latest sampler square and said, "I have an idea."

"Oh?"

"Can we move the old piano at Grey Gables outside?" she asked Annie. "If so, maybe Jason could play for us."

"That's a great idea!" Kate said. "I love piano music, especially live!"

"I like that suggestion," Annie said, "but I'm not sure about moving that huge old piano outside. Pianos are extremely heavy, you know, and where would we put it once we did get it out of the house? I need the porch for seating and to display Princessa jewelry."

"Don't worry about a thing," Peggy said. "I'll ask Wally to round up some of the men to move it, and I'm sure he can build you a small platform on the lawn."

Annie looked at her.

"Peggy, that would be wonderful, but would he have time? I know Wally is a busy man, and this would be extremely short notice."

Peggy grinned. "I'm sure it won't be a problem for him, Annie. You're one of his favorite people, you know. Besides me, that is. He'd do just about anything for either of us."

Everyone laughed, and Annie said, "Well, if he's willing to do it, that would be great. Will you have him call me so we can discuss it?"

"I will! As soon as the meeting is over."

"And speaking of the meeting being over," Mary Beth said, "it isn't. Is there any new business or news we need to discuss?"

Alice reached into her tote bag and pulled out all the sampler squares she'd made that week.

"Look!" she said. "I don't know if you'd call this 'news,' but I am so proud of myself."

"Look at that!" Peggy said. "You're doing great, Alice."

"You should be proud," Kate added, taking the squares and admiring them before she passed them around for the other woman to view. "I'm proud of you."

"Yes," Gwen said. "Learning a new craft is so rewarding."

"I agree, Gwen." Alice looked at Annie. "And having someone like Annie teaching me has been such a pleasure. Not only does she—"

"I have something to say," Stella announced in her most imperious voice, interrupting the exchange.

The group fell silent, and the women stilled their hands as they looked at her, waiting. Annie had learned long ago that when Stella spoke in that tone of voice, what she usually had to say was often serious and/or unpleasant. The fact that she interrupted Alice in mid-sentence underscored Stella's intent, whatever it was. The older woman fixed Annie with a steely expression, much the way a teacher would regard a problematic pupil.

"Annie, I see a major problem with your plan."

"Oh?" Right then, Annie had so many plans going on, she almost felt weighed down with them. "Which plan is that, Stella?"

"This plan for musical entertainment at your little … party." She made it sound as though Annie's cookout was going to be a haphazard, insignificant event. "You have not asked Jason to play."

Annie blinked.

"Oh, but I—"

"You just assumed he'd do this for you?"

Annie shifted beneath Stella's frown, keeping a lid on her temper by reminding herself of Stella's age and personality.

"Of course not," she said. "I would never presume to take advantage of him, and I have every intention of asking. I was hoping—"

"Hoping what? That I'd tell him to do it, and that would be that?" She waved a hand. "Jason has his own life, Annie Dawson."

Annie swallowed hard, feeling affronted and defensive. The prospect of Jason playing at the barbecue had just been proposed. Of course she liked Alice's idea and hoped that Jason would be willing to play the piano at her cookout. But she would never expect him to drop everything and do so simply because she asked, and she certainly wouldn't want Stella to order him to do it. Trust Stella Brickson to put this uncomfortable spin on the whole affair.

"I'll call Jason," she said, "but, Stella, please understand I need to find out first if having the piano outside is even doable. I don't want Jason to do this if he doesn't want to, and I certainly don't want to commit myself to such a feat if we can't use the piano. I may end up doing as Mary Beth suggested and set up a CD player somewhere."

Stella sniffed and pursed her lips. "Well," she said, and nothing else. She bent her head over the knitting in her hand.

After a few tense and extremely uncomfortable moments, Kate said, "Mary Beth, may we please talk about the music box now?"

"Of course!" Mary Beth looked at her shop assistant as if she had no idea why Kate asked such a thing.

The women shared a chuckle and the tense atmosphere began to dissolve. Stella seemed obviously interested in the music box, but just as obviously she kept that curiosity low-key. She glanced up as Annie reached into the large tote bag but quickly looked back at her knitting.

"Papa Dexter is a genius!" Annie declared as she pulled

out the music box. Stella's head snapped up.

"Alexander Dexter?" she said, eyes narrowed behind her glasses.

"Yes, that's him."

"Huh!" She muttered. She shifted in her chair, and jabbed her needle into a stitch as if she were angry at the knitted piece.

Annie and Alice exchanged a glance and silently agreed to talk about this later.

"Look, ladies," Annie said, drawing attention back to the music box. "I want to show you how this opens."

While relating the information Papa Dexter had given her about Malcolm Tyler's boxes, Annie demonstrated how to open the music box.

"See this butterfly?" she said, and they leaned forward en masse, squinting, as she held the box out. "Right here, under this wing ..." She pressed the hidden key, and the women gasped as the box came apart.

"Look at that!" Gwen said.

"I've never seen something like that before!" Kate said, peering closely. "Oh, my!"

Even Stella finally leaned in for a closer look.

"Last week," Annie said, "when we heard the rustling sound inside this box, it was the music manuscript, rolled neatly and tied in a ribbon, right here."

"Think of that!" Kate murmured, her eyes wide and sparkling.

"And best of all," Annie said, looking at every face in turn, "Papa Dexter fixed the movement. At first he thought it was jammed, but the music never played because this little part right here was damaged. The teeth had been broken off of this." She touched a fingertip to the bit of metal. "It's called a comb. Luckily, Papa had another music box that was broken, and he took the comb from it for this one."

"I guess it's called a comb because it looks like one," Peggy observed.

"Yes," Annie agreed. "I think so."

The women stared at the mechanism for a time, and then Kate said, "Would you please play it for us, Annie?"

"Yes, do!" said Mary Beth.

"Please!" added Gwen and Alice.

Stella had leaned back against her chair and resumed knitting at such an intensely high rate of speed, it seemed she would have finished her piece—and ten more just like it—before the meeting broke up. But when she looked up and met Annie's eyes, she nodded, briefly.

"Go ahead," she said. "Wind it up and play it, Annie."

Annie turned the key and a moment later the soft, light notes began to play while the tiny metal teeth of the comb struck each one.

Stella put down her work and listened, head tilted to one side like a bird in the spring.

When the music died, she met Annie's eyes again and said, "Isn't that the music Jason played from the composition you found in the music box?"

"Yes! Can you believe it?"

"Really?" Kate said, her eyes wider than ever. "You mean on the musical score?"

"Yes," Annie said.

"How great!" Peggy said. "But how ... odd."

"Very odd," Annie agreed.

"I don't understand," Stella said. "Why does it play that same tune?"

Annie shrugged. "I don't know. I wish I did. It just seems I uncover one piece of the puzzle only to discover another part is missing. One good thing has happened, though. I found out who had commissioned the music box, so maybe, if I can locate the man's family, they can enlighten me even further. At least searching for people is easier these days with the Internet, so maybe finding someone who knew Peter Starne won't be too difficult."

"Peter Starne?" Mary Beth and Gwen echoed in unison.

"Yes. I tracked down Malcolm Tyler's great-niece in Vermont. I called her, and she has a book in which all Malcolm's customers were listed, what they ordered and when. Peter Starne ordered that music box."

"Peter Starne, the piano tuner?" Mary Beth said.

Annie gawked at her. "Wh-what? You've heard of him?"

"Heard of him? Of course! Peter Starne was this area's best piano tuner," Gwen said. "He's in Seaside Hills Assisted Living now."

"He is?" Annie nearly squealed. "He's still alive?"

"Oh, yes," Mary Beth said, "he's in his nineties, quite frail physically, but his mind is still sharp as a tack."

Annie was so flabbergasted that she sat silently and stared at her companions.

"Do you mean to tell me the man who owned that music box is as close as Seaside Hills Assisted Living?"

"Unless there is another Peter Starne somewhere," Gwen said. "But I have a strong feeling he's the one. How many Peter Starnes are there in this part of the world, especially musical ones?"

"Then I must go see him!" Annie declared, ready to jump up immediately and hurry to the facility.

"For goodness sake! What a lot of fuss about so little." Stella jabbed her needle. "If he has lived this long, surely he will live long enough for you to see him in the home. You don't need to break your neck running out of here."

All the women gaped at her, and then exchanged glances with each other. Stella looked up and caught their expressions. She stopped working for a moment, her mouth a tight line. Finally her face softened.

"I apologize. That sounded cold," she said, her eyes clouding. "I'm often too blunt for my own comfort." She began to put her work away. "I'm sorry. Sometimes words just pour from my mouth without my permission, and they hurt whoever happens to be in the way. Today, I think we'd all be better off if I just go home."

"Oh, no!" Annie said. "Stella, don't leave. We understand. All of us say things without thinking sometimes."

"Of course we do," Mary Beth said.

No one added that Stella seemed to do it more than anyone else. She placed everything in her basket and got to her feet.

"Thank you for understanding, but I'm going to go now."

"Without Jason?" Gwen asked.

Stella paused at the door. "My driver is right down the street at The Cup & Saucer. I'll see you later, ladies."

"Stella!" Annie said as the woman opened the door. "You'll be at the cookout Saturday, won't you?"

"I don't know," Stella said after a moment's pause. Then she walked out, leaving her friends to puzzle after her.

Some of the shine was knocked off the day by Stella's peculiar behavior and careless words. Annie wondered what she had said or done that irritated the older woman, and how many times she would unknowingly irritate Stella in the future. She sighed loudly without realizing it.

"Oh, don't let her bother you," Peggy said. "You should know by now that Stella is a lovely woman who is full of good intentions. She doesn't seem to always be in tune with the rest of us."

"It's all right," Annie assured her concerned friends. "I believe I'm getting used to her. I know she's my friend." She glanced around. "The problem is, I just wish I knew when I'm getting under her skin before it happens."

"We all wish we knew how to do that," Mary Beth said. "I'm sure it all has something to do with that music you found. She got uncomfortable when you started talking about the music box and later about the party."

The meeting broke up, and various projects found their way back into tote bags or baskets. Everyone wanted to hear the music box again, so Annie played it again, and then they all left the store to go about the rest of their day.

~16~

Back home, Annie had barely stepped through her door when her phone rang. She half-expected to hear from Grady Brooks again, but caller ID told her the person on the other end was Wally Carson.

"Annie!" he said enthusiastically when she answered. "Good afternoon!"

"Hi, Wally," she replied with a laugh. "How are you? Did you get the library shelves finished?"

"I did. They look good too."

"I'm sure they do. You are a true pro, Wally. It's easy to see why your wife is your biggest fan."

He laughed. "I believe she is. And speaking of her, she tells me you need something built for your cookout this weekend, some kind of platform?"

"Yes, something level and strong to hold my piano. Can you do it?"

She could hear him take in a deep breath and let it out.

"Well, let me give it some thought, Annie. I'd surely like to do it for you, but I'm just not sure I can build it in the time we have left. Now if you can put off the barbecue a week or two …"

She knew he was teasing, trying to lighten the disappointment.

"I can't put it off, sorry to tell you. The invitations have been given, and Alice is baking up enough goodies to feed the entire Eastern Seaboard."

"As I said, let me give the matter some consideration, and I'll see what I can do about adjusting my schedule and commitments. Could be someone else might not mind waiting a few days."

"Oh, Wally, no. I don't want to inconvenience you or anyone else—"

"Now, Annie, listen to me. This is a great thing you're doing, throwing a big party for the whole community. I think the cedar lining for Mrs. Willingham can be pushed back to next week without undue inconvenience for anyone. I'll need to do some measuring and figuring first at your place before I start the platform. I'll stop by this evening, if that's all right?"

"Sounds good, Wally. Thank you!"

After a quick lunch, Annie freshened up, filled Boots's food and water bowls, and then fetched her purse and car keys. She was just stepping outside when the telephone rang again.

"Hi, Annie!" It was Alice. "Are you going to go see Peter Starne today?"

"I'm on my way right now. Well, actually, I'm going to go see Jason first. Wally called and said he thought he could build the piano platform for me. Would you like to go with me?"

"Annie, I would. I really, really would like to go with you, but today I'm elbow deep in cookie dough."

"Ooo! Sounds like fun."

"I like it. Maybe you should come over here instead of running around, seeing people, and solving mysteries."

They laughed together like two schoolgirls.

"Annie, I've been thinking," Alice said.

"Oh, now that sounds dangerous."

"Ha, ha—very funny. Seriously, though, I'm thinking that moving your big old piano is going to be hard, and moving it down the porch steps will make it worse. Plus, it's hard on a piano to be moved around a lot."

"Yes, I agree. Pianos are extremely heavy and unwieldy, but they are also delicate."

"And you don't want to give anyone a hernia," Alice added.

"Well, no. I'd rather not."

"I have a better idea than having that thing heaved all over the place."

Annie's interest piqued.

"Oh? And that would be … ?"

"Rather than having live music as a background all during the cookout, why not a just little mini-concert?"

Annie frowned. "But wouldn't that still involve moving the piano?"

"Only as far as the porch. We could have Jason—"

"If he'll do it," Annie said.

"Yes, if. And if he will, we could have him play some songs, and then when he's finished some of the guys can move the piano back into the house. This way, you won't have to get Wally to build a platform or a crew to haul the thing down the steps."

Annie mulled her friend's notion for a bit, liking the idea the more she thought about it.

"You might be on to something there, Alice. That would certainly simplify things, wouldn't it?"

"It would. And another thing."

"Yes?"

"I think you should display the music box. Believe it or not, it's caused a stir around town, and I think people would like to see it and learn more about it. I bet you'll be answering questions all day. Too bad you haven't gotten to the bottom of the puzzle about that unfinished sonata."

Annie heaved a sigh. "I know. I'd love to know who wrote it and where the rest of it is. But I do like your idea of displaying the music box. I just wish I had more to tell folks when they ask. If Peter Starne can't offer me much information, maybe someone else will before Saturday."

"I'll keep my fingers crossed, because that music is a true puzzle and very romantic."

"You are one hundred percent right. I'd like to meet this Olivia person. She must have been something else to have a sonata written for her—even if it is unfinished."

"I'd say so." Alice paused for just a moment, and then she asked, "By the way, have you heard from your old boyfriend again?"

"Oh, for heaven's sake!" Annie sputtered. "He said he'd like to come and if he does, he's bringing his friend from Portland. So get all these ridiculous matchmaking ideas out of your head, Alice. Grady and I have no romantic interest in each other whatsoever! And let's get something straight, you silly girl. Grady was not my boyfriend. Ever. And if he shows up, don't be all giggly and goofy about it. Please?"

Alice sighed so deeply Annie could nearly feel it through the telephone.

"All right. I'm just thinking of you and your happiness.

But you know something, Annie? You can be a real buzzkill."

"Yes. You've told me that before." She laughed a little at her friend's exaggerated sense of martyrdom. "Listen, I better get going. I have a lot to do, and so do you."

"OK. Let me know what Jason says, and what you learn from Mr. Starne."

"I will. Bye now."

When Annie arrived at Stella's home, the older woman's greeting at the front door was a little chilly, but completely courteous. She invited Annie into her sitting room, and once they were in there, she offered tea.

"Thank you, no," Annie said. "I just stopped by a moment to talk to Jason."

Stella's lips thinned. "About Saturday?"

"Yes." Annie saw no reason to engage in a dialogue that might end in with someone's feelings being wounded. She braced herself for more of Stella's resistance.

"I see. Well, let me go and get him. Please, Annie, have a seat while you wait."

A few minutes later Jason quietly entered the room alone. He gave her a warm smile.

"May I get you some coffee, Annie?"

"No, thanks, Jason. Do you have a minute to talk?"

"Sure." He sat down in a wing chair close to hers and looked at her with interest. "You seem tense, if you don't mind me saying so. Is there a problem?"

"No, no," she hastened to assure him. "Not at all. I'm afraid I might have irritated Stella a little earlier, though." She glanced at the doorway. "I guess that's why she's not here."

"Or maybe she's giving us privacy," Jason said. "Mrs. B

is a class-act lady, Annie, but I've learned it's best if you don't take her moods too seriously. She doesn't mean to be overbearing." He lost his smile and became rather business-like. "Is that what you wanted to talk to me about? Mrs. B? Because I don't feel comfortable talking about her."

"Not at all! Oh, goodness, no. I'm not here to gossip. I wanted to call on you for a favor of sorts."

"A favor?" He relaxed and smiled slightly. "All right. What is it you need?" He seemed so curious and uninformed that she was pretty certain Stella had not mentioned any-thing to him about Annie wanting him to play the piano at her cookout.

"You know I'm having a barbecue this Saturday at Grey Gables?"

"Oh, yes. We'll be there. Mrs. B is planning on bringing three dozen deviled eggs, and I'm going to bring a few bags of my world-famous potato chips."

She smiled. "Good! I appreciate all the help I've been getting, and I do believe there will be enough food to sink a ship."

"Let's not do that!" he laughed.

"No, let's not. Well, Jason, the favor has to do with the cookout."

"Oh? You want me to help you get things set up? It's going to take a lot of work to get tables and chairs in place, and I'll be happy to lend some muscle."

"Thanks for offering, but I think Ian and Wally and a couple of other men are coming early to get things set up. What I want from you is your talent."

He narrowed his eyes. "I beg your pardon?"

"I'd love for you to give us a piano concert. After the cookout."

He blinked.

"You're joking, right?"

"Not at all. Jason, I want some live music to make this a real party. I had scheduled the Nocturnal Loons band but Rory and Billy Flynn's grandfather passed away, and they had to cancel."

"I'm sorry to hear that. I never met him, but I understand he was a nice old gent. But Annie, I've never played at a party before."

"Don't look at it that way. Think of it as a recital. I'm sure you did recitals when you were a boy, didn't you?"

He rolled his eyes. "Twice a year for ten years, in front of friends and family, until I left home."

She grinned. "Then you know what's expected. I'd love for you to pick your favorite music and give us a recital. Just think how much everyone will enjoy it."

"Oh, I don't know …" He ran his fingers through his hair, chewed on his lower lip, and stared into the distance. He glanced at her as if expecting her to give him a reason not to, but she smiled back placidly and waited.

Finally he said, "Well, all right, then. I think I can do that."

At that very moment, Stella entered the room, the scent of her expensive perfume floating in the air, enveloping Jason and Annie with its powdery fragrance.

"Are you sure, Jason?" she asked, making no attempt to disguise her obvious eavesdropping. "Don't do this if you don't want to."

"Of course not, Jason," Annie chimed in. "I don't want you to participate if you really don't want to."

He looked back and forth between the two women for a moment.

"Sure I'm sure. It'll be fun." He smiled at Stella. "You'll let me practice on your piano, won't you?"

"Of course! Whatever you need." She turned to Annie. "So you've found someone to build you a platform and move that instrument outside, have you?"

"I talked to Wally and he agreed to do it, but since we're going to have a 'concert' instead of live music throughout the entire party, we won't need to take the piano any farther than the front porch. Alice suggested having a concert, and I believe it's a better idea."

"Indeed, yes. I assume you'll be paying Jason for doing this?"

Annie had not even considered a fee, and Stella's remark caught her off-guard.

"Well, certainly," she managed to say after a moment. "Whatever you think is fair, Jason."

"I think doing it for free is fair," he said. "I understand you're trying to help someone; let this be my contribution."

"Helping someone?" Stella said, looking at Annie narrowly. "Who are you helping? Not that wretched Alexander Dexter you mentioned the other day, I hope! He doesn't need—"

"Of course not. I'm just giving Alice's business a little boost. It's been a bit slow lately." She leaned forward slightly, meeting Jason's eyes, and then Stella's. "But this cookout is not a charity drive, and I trust neither of you will speak of it as such or treat it that way."

"Absolutely," Jason promised.

Stella smiled. "You show good sense, Annie."

"Thank you. I hope you are planning to come."

"Of course. I'd never miss the social event of the season in Stony Point."

"That's great. Papa Dexter asked if you'd be there."

Stella froze.

"Is that man going to attend?"

"I believe so, yes."

Stella huffed and walked from the room.

Annie gaped after her, and then looked at Jason who merely shrugged.

"Don't worry," he said. "She'll be there because she wouldn't miss hearing me play, even if Papa Dexter was singing and picking lead guitar."

As Annie drove to Seaside Hills Assisted Living, she kept puzzling why Stella had such a negative reaction to Papa Dexter when he seemed to hold her in high regard.

Oh, well, she thought, as she pulled into the parking lot of her destination. *That's Stella for you.*

— 17 —

Annie opened the front door of the Seaside Hills Assisted Living facility, grateful that the staff kept the place clean and inviting. With the music box in her tote bag, she passed through the large entry room. The jade green-and-gold rug, the soft pastoral prints on the walls, and comfortable chairs gave the big room a welcoming air. She smiled at the residents who looked up hopefully at her approach. As her glance passed over the wrinkled faces and bent bodies, she once again thought of Violet Hutchins' remarks about how little family history meant. And yet, look at the decades of history that were represented in this home—and in every similar facility across the country, in fact. How many of these dear old people had their own histories handed down and preserved?

Today, she was going to tap into one man's history, and she looked forward to it.

At the front desk, she waited until a red-haired young woman looked up from a computer keyboard.

"Hello," Annie said.

The girl got up, smiled, and approached her.

"Hi. How may I help you?"

"I'm looking for Peter Starne, and I understand he lives here."

The girl nodded. "He does. He's in the east wing, room

112. Would you like me to show you to his room, or can you find it?"

"I'm sure I can find it if you point me in the right direction," Annie said, and the girl indicated the hallway to her left.

"At the end of that corridor, turn right."

"Thank you."

Annie walked the shining white floor, passing the doors to offices, staff rooms, and the dining room. A glance into that room showed several clean, round tables with dispensers for salt, pepper, and napkins. At one table, eight white-haired women played a noisy game of cards. At another, a man and woman drank coffee and chatted, leaning toward each other like young lovers.

Annie smiled and kept walking. She turned right when the corridor intersected with another. She followed the hallway until she came to room 112. The door stood open. Daylight poured in through a large window. The room was pale green with white blinds, and there was a narrow bed with a white bedspread. Two small, green-and-tan easy chairs faced each other on either side of the window. A thin, white-haired man sat in one of the chairs, reading. He wore jeans, a long-sleeved pale blue shirt, and sneakers.

She knocked softly on the door frame. He looked up, clear dark eyes behind black-framed glasses, finger holding his place on the page. Surely this wasn't Peter Starne! Peter Starne was in his nineties, and this man looked to be no older than seventy-five, if that.

"Yes?" he said in a steady, strong voice.

"Are you Peter Starne?" she asked, taking a couple of steps into the room.

"I am." He regarded her with guarded curiosity. "Do I know you?"

"No, sir. My name is Annie Dawson. I'd like to speak with you, if I may?"

"If you're here to peddle trinkets or your religion, I already have enough doodads for this small space, and I attend worship services right here in the home."

"No, no," she said quickly, with a smile. "I'm not here to sell you anything or to convert you. But I'd like to talk to you about this."

She carefully pulled the music box from her tote bag.

The book he held slipped from his fingers and clattered loudly onto the tile floor. He stared in what seemed like horror at the wooden box in her hands. He shrank back in his chair as though trying to escape.

"Where ... where did you get that?" he asked weakly. "And why do you have it?"

"It was part of my grandmother's collection," she said, hurriedly setting the music box on the other chair. "Are you all right?"

When he did not respond, she turned toward the door, ready to dash down the corridor. "I'm going to call a nurse," she told him.

Peter Starne lifted one hand, but did not move his eyes from the box.

"Stay!" he said.

His eyes remained fixed on the music box for so long, Annie wondered if he had lost his thoughts. But after a lengthy time, he turned his gaze to her, his eyes a deep, liquid brown behind the lenses. It seemed he studied her for an eternity.

"You said that music box is part of your grandmother's collection," he said, finally. "Who is your grandmother?"

"Betsy Holden. She was an artist who lived here in Stony Point for a long time." She paused, and then added, "She passed away a while back."

He continued to scrutinize Annie as if he looked for some flaw in her appearance. She resisted the urge to check her hair with her hands. After a bit he seemed to return from whatever place he had traveled in his mind.

"Yes," he murmured. "I remember when she died. She was a fine woman."

Annie nodded. "The best."

"The resemblance to her is there," he said, "in your eyes. And maybe in the way you stand." He indicated the chair where she'd rested the music box and said, "Please. Sit."

Annie picked up the music box and sat on the edge of the chair, still watching him carefully, half-fearful that he was near collapse.

"Are you all right?" she asked again.

"I'm fine. But seeing that music box after all these years ... it gave me quite a turn."

She reached down, picked up his book from the floor and handed it to him.

"I am so sorry to have shocked you with it, Mr. Starne," she said, settling back into the chair. "I should have given you more warning."

He waved off her apology with one thin hand and shook his head. He placed a much-used bookmark between the pages of his book and set it aside on the small table near him.

"I never expected to see that box again, not after all this

time. In fact, I had asked Betsy to bury it for me."

"Bury it?" she echoed in shock.

"Yes. Or better still, burn it. But I see she ignored my request."

"Burn it?" Annie gazed down at the intricately carved music box again. "But it's so beautiful, so rare. In fact, these boxes carved by Malcolm Tyler are now collector's items." She turned back to Peter. "I don't understand why you'd want to give it away, let alone destroy it."

Instead of replying to that, he rubbed his palms along his thighs, as though rubbing away dampness. He said to her, "Would you hand it to me, please, miss?"

"Sure thing." Annie got up and held the music box out to him.

He stared at it while she stood, unmoving, holding it out to him in both hands. Peter ran his fingers across the velvety dark wood, touched the vines, the lovebirds, and lastly, traced the heart with a fingertip. At last he took it from her, his hands shaking.

"Is it too heavy for you?" she asked. "I don't mind continuing to hold it while you look at it."

"It's not too heavy." He settled the box in his lap, gazing at it, stroking it with tender hands. He lifted the top lid and examined the empty compartment. "This was to hold gold and diamonds—rings, necklaces, bracelets."

"Oh?" Annie said, almost in a whisper as she seated herself again. But she doubted he would have heard her, even if she had shouted. It seemed Peter had forgotten she was there, and she was content to wait until once more he mentally returned to the room where they sat.

After a while, he lifted the box and shook it.

The wrinkles on his brow deepened and he shook it again, head tilted to one side as though listening. He lifted his gaze and gave her a sharp look.

"What happened to it?" he asked.

She raised her eyebrows. "What do you mean?"

"You know what I mean! My sonata! If it were still inside I would hear it move when I shake the box. The sonata was supposed to be sealed inside and never removed. It was supposed to be destroyed along with this box! What happened to it?"

He shoved the music box toward her, and she grabbed it mere seconds before it would have crashed to the floor.

His entire body trembled—lips, hands, legs. His eyes clouded with unshed tears.

"Why did you bring this to me?" he cried. "Why must I live it all again?"

He gripped the arms of his chair so hard his knuckles shone large and white, and he turned his face to the window, staring hard at the world beyond his room.

"Mr. Starne," Annie said, feeling sick. "Please, sir, my purpose in coming here and in bringing this box was not to cause you pain."

His gaze remained focused outside for what seemed ages, and then he finally turned his head to face her.

"Then why have you come, like a wraith, to haunt me in my last days? Why did your grandmother betray my trust by preserving that ... that awful piece of history?" His eyes found the box once more.

Annie felt worse than ever.

"Believe me, Mr. Starne, when I tell you again that my intention was not to upset you, or to destroy your peace of mind."

"I trusted Betsy Holden," he muttered. "I did not expect her to betray me."

The words stung, and Annie leaped to her grandmother's defense.

"Please don't even think such a thing," she said. "Gram kept this lovely and rare music box because she was a keeper of treasures—a steward of something that has no equal. In her mind, to destroy something as beautiful as this music box would have been the real betrayal."

He glared at her, at the box, and turned to face the window again. He said nothing. Perhaps, Annie thought, she should leave. Staying might cause him more pain. And yet she could not go until he understood that Gram had appointed herself as caretaker of a mystery rather than having gone back on an agreement.

"If it makes you feel any better," she said softly, "Gram kept the music box with a collection of others, and this one stayed on the top shelf. She never let me touch it, and she never displayed it overtly for others to examine."

After a moment, he said in a rasp, "Where's the manuscript I hid in that box? It was never again to see the light of day."

She hesitated, and then said, "I have it."

He glanced at her, running his gaze over her head to toe, as if he expected her to have it in her pocket. "Where do you have it?"

"It's at home, in my desk, in a folder."

He grunted and looked out the window again.

"You have no right to keep it."

"I'll be happy to bring it to you, Mr. Starne. It's a lovely piece of music."

He snapped his head around and fixed a steely look on her. "You've heard it?"

"Yes. And the movement inside the music box has been repaired—"

He tried to stand up, gripping his chair for support.

"You had no right to do that!" he yelled. "What business is it of yours? You have no right to resurrect the dead!"

Annie could only gape silently at him. A young woman in pale blue scrubs and white, thick-soled shoes rushed into the room. She held a half-eaten candy bar in one hand and a paperback book in the other.

"What's all the commotion? Peter, are you all right?"

The man said nothing, but continued to glare at Annie.

"What did you say to him?" asked the woman. The little black and white pin she wore said her name was Corliss.

"I didn't mean to upset him," Annie said, all but wringing her hands. "Mr. Starne, I am so sorry." She spoke to Corliss again, pointing at the music box. "I only wanted some information about this antique music box that once belonged to Mr. Starne."

Corliss put down her candy and her romance novel. She glowered at Annie.

"I must ask you to leave," she said as she lifted Peter's wrist and tested his pulse.

"Certainly," Annie said meekly. "I am so sorry, truly."

"You should be! Coming into a place where people are

trying to have some peace and causing this disturbance," said Corliss.

Feeling lower than she had in a long time, Annie shoved the music box back in the protective tote. She was almost out the door, blinking back tears of frustration and embarrassment when Peter spoke again.

"No!" he said. She turned to see him tugging his arm free of the hovering orderly. "No, I want to talk with Betsy's granddaughter."

Annie stopped in her tracks, shocked by this reversal of attitude. "You do?"

Corliss regarded him from cool blue eyes. "Are you sure?"

"I do, and I am." He fixed his steely gaze on Corliss. "Will you excuse us, please? And pardon us for disturbing you when you were so ..."—he glanced at her candy bar and book—" ... busy."

Annie wondered if she was the only one to hear the irony in his tone. Apparently so, because Corliss patted the old man's shoulder, glared at Annie, and then grabbed up her food and reading material, and trotted off to take care of other things.

"I certainly seem to have caused some upset to everyone," she said.

He fixed his gaze on Annie again. "You caused me some upset," he said, "but don't worry about Corliss. Why, she's the laziest girl here. I don't believe I've ever seen her without a candy bar. It must be like a pacifier to her."

Annie met his eyes.

"Whether I've upset her or not, it's you I'm concerned for. If I'd known how you felt, I certainly would never have—"

He waved off her words. "I'm an old man. It's time to put the past behind me rather than hiding from it, I think. Obviously you are the instrument that is supposed to help me do that."

She was not sure how to respond to his fatalistic attitude, so instead she said, "Mr. Starne, I appreciate your willingness to talk to me."

He drew in a deep breath and let it out slowly. "If I'm going to talk, I'll need water. Would you mind pouring me some, please?"

"Of course." She started to pour water from a gray plastic pitcher into a matching gray cup. "Mr. Starne, this water is room temperature. Wouldn't you prefer some that is fresh and cool?"

"To tell you the truth, I'd prefer a nice cold cola, but I don't get one very often."

She smiled. "I saw a vending machine in the lobby. How about if I go get you a cola?"

His eyes lit up. "I'd like that!"

"All right. I'll be right back."

When she returned, she said, "While I was out, I popped into the dining room and requested a bigger cup for you and some ice."

He smiled and watched as she opened the can and poured the sparkling brown drink over chunks of ice. It foamed, whispering, nearly to the top of the cup.

She pulled a straw free from its wrapper, inserted it into the drink, handed the cup to him and said, "I told Corliss you needed a fresh pitcher of cold water, not something tepid from the tap."

For the second time his eyes lit up. "You did? Nobody ever tells Corliss anything! Good for you, Mrs. ... Mrs. ... what did you say your name was?"

"Annie Dawson. Please call me Annie."

"I'll do that." He took a sip of his soda and smiled. "Ah," he said after the first drink. "That's good!" He dipped his head in the direction of the other chair. "Sit down, please. People who hover like the angel of death make me jumpy."

Unaware that she had been "hovering," Annie meekly sat down.

Peter sipped his cola until she was sure most of it had gone down his throat.

"Why don't you have soda pop very often? Especially since there is a machine so close."

He burped discreetly, apologized, and then said, "Doctor says I'm not supposed to have it."

Annie felt her eyes widen.

"Then why did you ask for it?" she asked in dismay.

"I didn't ask for it. I just said I'd like to have one. You ran out of here to get it for me, and you didn't even bother to ask if I could have it or not." He took another deep drink, and then grinned at her wickedly.

"Why ... why ... you brat!"

He laughed out loud at that.

"Give me that cup!" she reached for it, and he sucked down the last so fast and hard that the straw flushed noisily against the bottom of the cup.

"Oh, my." She got up. "I better get Corliss."

He grabbed her arm before she'd taken two steps.

"Don't bring that ninny back in here. The only reason

the doc doesn't want me to have soda is because he wants me to drink more water." He held out the cup. "Pour that water over the ice, and I'll put everyone's mind at ease."

She did what he asked, but realized Peter was sharp, quick, and witty. He was an elder who belied the stereotype of nursing-home residents. Annie sat down again and met his twinkling eyes.

"Mr. Starne, I really, really did not come here to cause you pain. If you want me to go, I fully understand."

His smile slid away, and he replaced the twinkle with something somber. Annie regretted returning to the subject that minutes ago had caused such raw, unbridled emotion.

"I know that, miss," he said. "I can tell by your eyes and your manner that you are a lady inside and out."

"Thank you." Relief flushed through her. "Thank you."

Peter set the cup next to his book. Interlacing his fingers and resting his hands in his lap, he gave his attention to Annie.

"I won't pretend you haven't surprised me by showing up with it," he told her quietly, "but please tell me: Why have you brought the music box to me? What have you done with the music that was in it, and why do you feel it necessary to extract something that had been hidden away?"

So he wasn't as amenable as he had seemed. In fact, his old eyes were sharp and taking in every blink, every breath, and every movement she made.

Annie smoothed her hair as if she were auditioning for a part in a play. She cleared her throat and glanced down at the music box. She lightly rubbed the flat of her hand across it, feeling the pattern of the carvings.

"I have found a lot of puzzling treasures in Gram's house since I moved to Stony Point," she told him. "All of them have been special in different ways. In tracking down the mysteries behind these items, I've learned about this town, this state, my grandmother, and myself. Mr. Starne, this music box," she patted it tenderly, "is another puzzle that needs to be unraveled and put back together."

He moved restlessly.

"I don't understand why you need to know anything about that box."

She studied him, looking into the old eyes that, while clear, seemed haunted somehow, as if they carried the weight of an unhappy life. How sad it must have been to live to this advanced age with a secret so devastating that he wanted to destroy such a rare masterpiece.

Annie leaned forward and rested her hand on one of his.

"Mr. Starne, don't you think it's time to uncover the past and release it to the light of day? Haven't you borne this burden from the past long enough?"

He looked at her and his mouth quivered. A single tear slid down his creased face. He turned his hand and gripped Annie's.

"Yes," he whispered. "It's time. I'll tell you my story."

~ 18 ~

"Can't I stay home?" a six-year-old Peter Starne asked his mother. "I know my ABCs and how to write my name and how to count to a hundred."

Mrs. Starne smiled down at her blond-haired, dark-eyed son, handed him a brown sack with a ham sandwich wrapped in a clean, white cloth.

"It is the first day of school; you must go," she told him.

"I'd rather stay home and play the piano."

"I know, son," she said, stroking his hair. "You play the piano so well, and I know how much you love it. But playing the piano will not help you get a job when you grow up. You must also learn to read and write and do your sums."

"But can I play my songs when I get home?"

She ruffled his hair. "Yes, you may. Now, scoot. You don't want to be late on your first day."

Before he stepped out the door, he looked up at her soberly and said, "When I grow up, I will get a job where I play the piano all the time!"

She smiled and watched his small figure join his waiting older brother and sister at the gate. When he reached them, Peter turned around and waved to her.

"You'll like school," said Ida, his sister, as she took his lunch bag and carried it for him as they walked. "You'll meet lots of other children."

"Yeah, squirt," his brother Arthur said. "You need to play with kids, not just pianos."

Peter said nothing. He knew he would not like school if it had no piano. But maybe it would. He remembered seeing an old woman play the piano at Ida's school program last year. He brightened and walked along, a little happier for the moment.

That happiness lasted only until he, Ida, and Arthur entered the building of Halstead, Michigan's, elementary school. Ida took him to the door of a room filled with boys and girls his age, while Arthur ran on to another room.

"After school," Ida said, handing him his lunch, "wait for me at the door where we came in." Then she gave him a quick kiss on the cheek. "Have fun, Petey."

Peter watched his sister walk away and join a couple of friends who waited for her at the foot of a flight of steps. The three girls, in fresh haircuts and new clothes, ran giggling upstairs.

"Come in, little boy," said a kindly voice, and he turned. A lady who looked as nice as his mother and smelled like the talcum powder she used smiled at him.

"What's your name?" she asked.

"Peter Christian Starne."

"It's nice to meet you, Peter. I'm Miss Carey, your teacher." With her hand on his shoulder, she led him into the classroom.

Some of the other children glanced at him, but most of them were busy looking at their desks, or new pencils and tablets, or the pictures of presidents on the wall. Above the blackboard behind the teacher's big desk at the front of the room the alphabet had been painted in bright red letters.

He pointed at them.

"I already know my ABCs," he said.

"That's wonderful!"

He glanced around.

"Don't you have a piano?"

She laughed softly and patted his head. "No, not in this room. But we do have a piano in the music room."

"Can I play it now?"

She gave him a sad smile.

"I'm sorry, Peter. We have music only on Fridays."

"Can I play it then?"

She shook her head. "You children sing, and Mrs. Pratt plays the piano."

Peter heaved a sigh. School would be worse than he imagined if he never got to play the piano, not even once a day.

"Now," Miss Carey was saying, "this is your desk. And this is your desk mate, Olivia Sloan. Olivia, this is Peter Starne."

Olivia, seated silently and serenely at the desk rather than examining the room like most of the other pupils, turned her head to look at him. She had shining black hair with lovely bangs that hung above eyes that were bluer than an April sky. With long, thick lashes, a small nose, and cherry lips, Olivia Sloan was by far the prettiest girl Peter had ever seen. He stared and stared at her. When she smiled shyly at him, she had two deep dimples, one adorning each cheek.

Without saying a word, Peter sat beside her and gave her a nervous little smile.

"Hello," she said, her dimples peeking.

"Hi," he muttered. He looked away from her because

she kept smiling at him as if she wanted him to talk to her, and he couldn't think of a thing to say. He wanted to tell her how pretty she was. He wanted to say he was happy they were sitting together. He wanted to ask her if she liked music, and if she could play the piano. Instead, all those words just jumbled up in his head and nothing came out.

"I'm a little scared," she said softly. He turned his head and saw her clench and unclench her hands as she chewed on her lower lip. "Are you scared too?" she asked him.

More than anything, Peter did not want his lovely new friend to be afraid. He thought if he acted brave and smart, she would feel better.

"Nah," he said. "There's nothing to be afraid of here."

She showed her dimples again. "Really? OK, then." She put her hand on his, "But you be my friend all day, in case I get scared again, OK?"

Her soft, warm hand on his made him feel all light and bouncy inside. He nodded.

"OK." And he didn't say anything else because he was too overwhelmed.

A loud bell rang, and Miss Carey stood in front of the class, smiling.

"Welcome to the first day of first grade," she said. "You children have just taken a big, brave step into a new world."

As the school years passed, Olivia and Peter almost always sat near one another, though at recess, Peter played ball or rolled hoops with the boys, and Olivia played quieter games such as jacks or house with the girls. Sometimes the other children teased them because, at their age, boys and girls simply were not friends. Peter didn't care if he was teased, and neither did Olivia. To them, their pairing was more natural than the sun rising and setting daily.

Olivia became all the more beautiful as they grew up. Peter's interests remained focused on his music and on his Olivia. When he wasn't at his piano, he was with her, and they walked hand-in-hand through their small town, looking in shop windows, pausing to play tag or blindman's bluff with other children. As a young teenager, Peter continued to ignore teasing about his devotion to a girl and to music. They were the true loves in his life, and he'd rather cut off both legs than to be without either one.

By the time they were in high school, teachers recognized Peter's talent and encouraged his parents to send him to a music conservatory where he could learn theory and composition. Their reluctance grew as the dark days of the Great Depression lingered. Money was scarce, of course, but more than that, they feared an education in music created a career doomed to failure.

"I can teach. I can compose. I can perform!" Peter argued hotly when his mother and father repeated their concerns. He added, somewhat bitterly, "If nothing else, I can tune pianos, but thanks for your faith in me."

His desire to pursue music was so strong that Peter began taking odd jobs, hoping to alleviate his parents' financial worries. He cut grass in his neighbors' yards or delivered groceries for the local market. Often, he ran errands for some of the older women in town. Seeing his relentless pursuit of this dream, Peter's mother and father finally and reluctantly gave him their blessing and he applied to several music schools.

Olivia shared his enthusiasm and his dream. Each week

she gave him the few cents she had earned by washing dishes or ironing for her mother.

"We'll travel the world," she told him one evening as they strolled, arm in arm, down the quiet, tree-lined avenues of Halstead. "You will perform for great crowds. I—and our children, of course—will sit in the audience of every performance and applaud for you louder than anyone!"

"Won't you get tired of hearing me play?"

She had squeezed his arm tightly. "Never! I haven't gotten tired of it yet, have I?"

He had never asked her to marry him, nor had she asked him. It was simply a fact they both knew, like knowing they would graduate soon, or sit down to supper each evening. With a sense of inevitability, in the spring of their senior year they began to plan a simple June wedding. It was a complete surprise to both of them when both sets of parents formed a committee of sorts, and called them into the front parlor of the Sloans' large, elegant home. The four elders sat, serious and implacable.

Olivia's father, a tall, dark-haired man with a firm jawline and hard mouth, announced no union would occur between the two young people—at least not for a long time.

Peter and Olivia were stunned. She turned large blue eyes to him, clutching his arm.

"Peter?" she cried.

"Of course we're going to get married!" he said, gripping Olivia's hand. "As soon as we graduate and find a place to live." He looked at the others. "We have known this since first grade. Why would any of you believe otherwise?"

"We have always known you would pursue music," his

mother said. "That is what we've always known."

"Yes," his father agreed. "How can you expect to support a family and attend the music conservatory at the same time? Because let me tell you, son, if you and Olivia were to marry, a family will surely come, and quickly. You must complete your education, and then set out to earn a living. Then you may think about getting married."

"No!" he and Olivia cried together, almost frantic.

"Olivia," her father said, "you have never dated any other boy but Peter. How do you know he is the man you want to be with for the rest of your life? You need to meet other young men before you settle down. You've always had what you wanted, and we've always given you the best. A musician's salary will be, at best, minimal."

"I don't care!" she shouted. "I plan to get a job while Peter is in college."

"And where would you get this job that would pay enough to support the two of you and any babies that come along during those years?"

Olivia gulped.

"There are all kinds of dress shops in Minneapolis. I can work there, or a five-and-dime, or even in a grocery store. We'll be together and that's what's important."

"Oh, darling!" her mother said. "Retail! Really? You don't want to work in retail. You'd be on your feet all day, and people would treat you like a servant. We'll happily send you to Miss Jane Masters Advanced Academy for Young Women. In fact, we've already sent off the paperwork, and you've been accepted."

Olivia's eyes grew big. "But that's in Atlanta, Georgia,

Mother! I told you a hundred times I won't go. It's a million miles from here. I won't go. I won't! Peter," she said, turning to him, panic on her pale face, "I won't go!"

"I know," he said quietly, slipping an arm around her. "I won't let you."

"I hardly think you can stop her, young man," Mr. Sloan said. "She will be leaving the week after graduation."

"I won't!" Olivia shrieked.

"You will."

Peter's parents stoically sat in the Sloans' living room, saying nothing to stop this disastrous state of affairs. In fact, by their mere lack of action or words to stand up for his beloved, he felt completely overwhelmed and bitterly betrayed.

"You can't send her away," he said. "She has her own life to live."

Mr. Sloan rounded on him, fury in his eyes. "That is what we are trying to accomplish, young man! We want to give her an opportunity to have a life before she ties herself down to a house, a husband, and children." He softened his expression and his voice. "You children don't seem to understand that you won't be young forever. There is plenty of time for marriage and the responsibilities it brings, but these are the days for you to explore the world and find out what it is you really want."

Olivia stood. "I want to marry Peter!" she shrieked. "It's all I've ever wanted, and you know that!"

He got to his feet also. "And all I have ever wanted was to have my music and to be with Olivia. Nothing else will do."

"Peter," his mother said softly, "think about what you just said."

He looked at her, waiting for her to continue.

"You just said that all you wanted was to have your music and be with Olivia."

"Yes. And I meant it."

Everyone was silent.

"Honey," his mother said, "do you realize you put your music first?"

"That's right," Mrs. Sloan chimed in. "Music before Olivia."

For a moment their words were nothing more than a jumble of foolish prattle that hummed irrationally in his brain. He looked from face to face to face, and lastly settled on Olivia's. Her wide eyes searched his, questioning, pleading, until the impact of what he had said reached his sense of reason.

"I love them both," he stammered, "music and Olivia, Olivia and music. I love them and want them both."

"But you put music before Olivia," his father said, "and whether you realize it or not, that is how your priorities lie."

"Exactly!" Mr. Sloan put in. "That is why we cannot allow you children to marry so young. Peter, you must follow your chosen career. You've worked for it. Your parents have sacrificed to give you the needed education." He walked to his daughter, resting his hands on her shoulders as he looked into her eyes. "Olivia, darling, you must be certain you are content to come second in Peter's life because, believe me, it will always be so. An artist's work will always come first. If it doesn't, his life falls into unhappiness at best and a shambles at worst. We want what is best for you—what will make you happy. Give yourself time to consider all this."

Olivia stood, frozen in place, staring at her father. "You're wrong, Papa," she said. At last she turned and met Peter's eyes. She swallowed hard and whispered, "You would give up your music for me, wouldn't you, if you had to?"

He stared at Olivia, hardly believing the words that came from her—the person who knew him better than anyone. How could she ask such a thing?

"Olivia … I could no more give up music than I could give up you!"

"But if you had to, would you?"

"But I don't have to, so why would you ask?"

"Peter!" Her eyes searched his, and then filled with tears. "Peter!"

"Why would you ask me such a thing?" he asked, his own voice tortured with confusion and hurt.

She gasped as though needing air. She ran from the room, from the interference of the adults in her life—and she ran from him.

The day after high school graduation, Olivia left home without protest to enter Miss Jane Masters Advanced Academy for Young Women. She went away, leaving a cool kiss on Peter's cheek and without shedding a tear. In the weeks before she left, Peter had tried to mend their fractured relationship. He visited, he brought gifts, he wrote notes, but she was like someone he'd never seen before. She was polite, reserved and completely detached as if she had lost all feeling for him—but when he chanced to look deeply into her eyes, he knew she still loved him.

He also knew all it would take to win her back was to declare he would give up his music for her. Peter felt, deep in his soul, if he ever spoke those words aloud they somehow would become a self-fulfilling prophecy. If he gave up music for Olivia, then what could he offer her? Music was all he had, and without it, he was nothing. He began to write his longing into a sonata for her, pouring his heart into the sweet, solemn notes.

In the fall, Peter went to the Bracken Institute of Music in Minneapolis. He studied music history and theory, composition, instrument construction and maintenance. The list of classes he hoped to take seemed like a golden street to him, leading him onward. His heart ached for Olivia, but throwing himself headlong into study kept him busy—body, mind, and soul. In those rare, spare moments he found, he worked on the sonata he had started at home, the one Olivia's absence had stirred in him. He wrote to her often. Sometimes she replied with a brief note. Other times, he heard nothing in response. Peter was determined to win her back the moment he was out of school.

Minneapolis was several hundred miles from Halstead, Michigan. He made the journey back only once that first year, at Christmas. Olivia had gone to London with two of her friends from Miss Jane Masters Academy, and he felt his heart bleed.

In his second year at Bracken, he spent an early summer weekend at one of the lakes with a friend. They rented a small, primitive cabin and spent those few days fishing, swimming, and talking about music. Peter took a solitary walk early one evening along the shoreline. He came across a scruffy, bearded man sitting next to the lake's edge, a small fire crackling beside him with a coffeepot in the coals. The smell of scorched coffee was unpleasant, and Peter started to hurry past when he noticed the old fellow whittling a block of wood. A closer look proved the man was not whittling, but was actually carving.

"Did you bring yourself a cup?" the man said, not looking up.

"Huh?" Peter said, confused by the question until he realized the other fellow was talking about a coffee cup. "No, sir. Thank you. I'm just taking a walk."

The man did not reply as he continued to work on the wood. The early evening light created shadows along the crevices and thin lines he carved, and Peter could not help but be drawn into the creation of what was before him.

"What are you making?" he said as he took a step closer.

"A box."

"May I watch?"

The man said nothing, and Peter decided if he wasn't welcome there he'd be dismissed. He squatted and watched the thin blade tenderly coax tiny pieces of wood from the block. A deft twist here, a languid stroke here, and the pattern of the far shoreline took place before his eyes.

"That's beautiful!" he said softly. "How do you do it?"

Silence held for a time, and then the man said, "It's what I do."

How long Peter sat there watching, he didn't know. It was completely dark with nothing but the light of the campfire, but the carver continued, as if he could see with his fingertips.

"I write music," Peter said, finally.

For the first time, the man looked up. His eyes glittered

in the firelight. He was not the old relic Peter had first believed. In fact, he was probably in his early or mid-thirties. He simply looked at Peter for a long time, and then turned back to his work.

"Well, I guess I'll be going now," Peter said after a while. The man did not respond, and Peter stood. "Thanks for letting me watch. It's fascinating."

The man nodded only enough to indicate he knew Peter had spoken.

"Good night." Peter knew the wood-carver would not respond, and he made his way back to the cabin.

That night Peter dreamed that Olivia was standing next to the lake, looking to the other side, and that, even though he called and called to her, she could not hear him. At the point of giving up, he started to turn from her when at his feet he saw a box. He picked it up, and the music of his sonata seemed to rise, touching the trees, and kept rising higher until the air and even the stars were infused with it.

He woke up suddenly. The first rays of sunlight were threading their way through the gaps in log walls of the cabin. It was so clear to him right then how to get his Olivia back. Peter would waste no time implementing his plan. His friend lay snoring in his sleeping bag across the small room and did not stir when Peter got up and slipped outside into the cool freshness of the new morning.

He retraced his steps along the lakeshore. He did not know where the wood-carver lived, but he was determined to find him. It didn't take long. The man was stirring his campfire in the same spot Peter had found him the night before. He glanced at Peter.

"You bring a cup this time?" he asked.

The question surprised Peter. He laughed unexpectedly and sobered just as fast.

"No. I didn't think of it. Sir? I'm here to talk to you about your carving."

"I don't take students." He carried the coffeepot to the lake where he dumped yesterday's remains.

"I'm not asking for lessons," Peter said. "I want you to carve a music box for me. Can you do that?"

The wood-carver squatted and rinsed out his coffeepot.

"I've made 'em," he said.

"Will you make one for me?"

It seemed an eternity while the man filled the pot with water and carried it back to the campsite. He measured coffee into it and put it in the coals. From a small bundle of what looked to be a bedroll, he took out a small notebook and pencil. He moistened the tip with his tongue.

"Tell me your name and what you want."

***

In early November, Peter carefully drafted a letter to Olivia, asking to see her at Christmas.

"We've been apart almost two years by now," he had written. "My education is nearly over, and soon I'll be able to provide a home for you, if you still want me. Please, Olivia, I ask that you give us an opportunity to reclaim what you and I both know is our true destiny. If you are amenable, I will call on you during Christmas week. This time, let us endeavor to heal what has broken between us."

The letter he received from her was warmer than previous missives, but not the effusive response he'd hoped for.

"I'm willing to see you during Christmas vacation. Please call ahead of time. Thank you."

Peter moved through the following weeks in a flurry of schoolwork, classes, recitals, and final exams. His heartbeat sped every time he thought of seeing Olivia again, but his time was so consumed with his education that opportunity to ponder or prepare for reuniting with her was scant.

On December 2, the wood-carver—Malcolm Tyler was his name—showed up at the front door of the dormitory where Peter lived. He looked the same as when Peter first met him, except perhaps shabbier and thinner. He exchanged an exquisite music box for the sum of money he'd required, an amount that Peter hardly believed could last the man a week. He had added as much as he could spare and gave it to Tyler in an envelope.

"It's ready for the music movement to be fitted into it," Tyler said, and showed Peter how to open the box by pressing beneath a butterfly's wing on the side. And without another word, he slipped off into the night.

The next morning, Peter took the box into the city to the experienced metalsmith who had crafted the music movement. Although his sonata was unfinished, he had written enough that the smith was able to make a movement that played the introduction. When the music box was complete with the intricate carvings and the delicate sound of his sonata coming from within, Peter knew he had commissioned the perfect gift to offer his Olivia. Surely she would see his very heart in this offering and forgive him for having two loves in his life. Surely she would understand.

That night, he used what little money he had left after paying for his extravagant gift and made a long distance call to Miss Jane Masters Advanced Academy for Women.

The voice of the young woman who answered the call was subdued, almost somber. When the operator said, "Sir, you may speak now," Peter eagerly asked for Olivia Sloan.

"I beg your pardon?" said the solemn young woman on the other end of the line.

"May I speak with Olivia Sloan?" he repeated. "Please tell her it's Peter calling."

There was such a long silence that he grew agitated.

"Hello? Hello? Is anyone there?" he practically shouted into the cone-shaped mouthpiece.

"Yes, I'm here," came a strangled-sounding voice. "I'm sorry. A moment please."

"This is long distance," he said. "Please, would you get Olivia Sloan for me?"

"Sir? Sir, I'm so sorry to t-tell you …" There was the unmistakable sound of a sob. "I'm sorry, but Olivia was k-killed in an auto accident this afternoon."

"What?" When she continued to sob, he shouted, "What? What was that? I don't believe you! I don't believe you!"

And then he did. The truth slammed into him with the ferocity of a sucker punch. He dropped the receiver from his hand and slumped against the wall.

That night, two weeks before the end of the semester, Peter left Bracken Institute and never returned. He did not return to the state of Minnesota, and he never saw his home or family in Michigan again.

~ 19 ~

When Peter Starne finished telling Annie of his life, his eyes were so full of pain she could hardly bear to look back at him.

"I am so sorry," she said.

"It was my fault she died," he told her, "and I have lived my life knowing that."

"Mr. Starne," Annie said, laying her hand on his. "You know you had nothing to do with her death. How could you when you were in Minnesota, and she was in Georgia?"

He shook his head and pulled his hand free of hers.

"If I had not put music ahead of her, if she had been my first love, my only love, we would have spent the rest of our days together."

"Oh, but—"

"I knew Olivia; I knew her better than anyone else, even her parents. If I had told her she meant more to me than my music, she would not have consented to go to that women's college so far away, no matter what her father would have said or done. She would have stayed right there in Halstead and waited for me. Or, more likely, we would have run off together after graduation and been married. But I broke her heart, and she left me."

He swallowed hard, and his hands shook. Annie took his cup from the table, poured him some fresh water and gave it to him. She waited until he drained the cup.

"I gave up my fancy dreams, Annie," he said. "How could I follow such a life, knowing the price that had been paid? That night, I vowed never to return to my first love. See how I still call music my 'first love?' Olivia should have always been my first love. So, I became a piano tuner and nothing more."

"Oh, Mr. Starne," Annie murmured. Her heart ached for him. "The world undoubtedly missed out on one of the most gifted American composers of the twentieth century."

He shook his head. "Musicians come and go, but there was only one Olivia."

"I'm so sorry," she whispered, wishing she knew something to say that would make him feel better, but she didn't.

"The sonata—the one I wrote for Olivia," Peter Starne said. "It's not unfinished. I finished it, but only in my mind. I could never write down another note of music after she died. I still hear it—that sonata—day after day. It haunts me like the ghost of my unhappy love."

"It's a beautiful piece," Annie told him. "It stirred me when I heard it. It made me long for … I'm not sure exactly how it happened, but it made me long for my late husband."

He nodded. "Yes. It's that kind of music."

She picked up the music box.

"Did you break off the comb on the movement?"

"I did. And then I took the score of the unfinished sonata and put it into the secret compartment in the bottom of the box." He fixed his eyes on the box. "For forty years, I kept that thing with me. I thought if I got rid of it—if I buried it or destroyed it—maybe I could bury or destroy the past and bring some peace to my soul. By that time, I was living in Stony Point. No one knew my life's story. I was just the piano tuner. I struck up a friendship with your grandmother, and when I realized I could not destroy the box or the sonata myself, I asked her to do it for me."

"And she agreed to destroy it?"

"She said she would 'take care of it.' I thought she would destroy it, since that's what I'd asked."

Bitterness crept into his voice, and Annie rushed to soothe him.

"As I said before, Gram was a steward of things, not a destroyer. And she basically did what you wanted: She took it from your sight and put it in a place where you no longer had to deal with it." She paused, letting her words sink in. "Am I right?"

He sighed. "Yes. Yes, of course, you are." He met her eyes. "I suppose on some level I knew she could never burn it or bury it. Maybe I just needed to hand it over."

"Yes," Annie said. "Hand it over. And now, Mr. Starne, you need to hand over your guilt and your despair. You've mourned your Olivia, but you've gone beyond that. By taking on the burden of her death, you haven't allowed her to rest. That's why you continue to feel haunted and miserable."

He stared at her, his eyes searching her face almost frantically, as if searching for hidden deception and cruelty.

"Do you think so, Annie? Do you really believe that?"

She reached out again, grasped his hand, and this time he held on.

"I absolutely, positively believe it. You are a good man. You have lived an honorable life. It's time to take another step and forgive yourself."

Tears filled his eyes, and he clutched her hand with both of his.

"I want to! I want to more than anything."

"Then it can be done."

* * *

Annie woke up at dawn on Saturday. The first thing she did was to look out the window and greet the clear sky with gratitude. She hoped the entire day passed with a bright blue sky and warm golden sunlight. The last thing she—or Alice—needed was a stormy, rainy day.

She had invited Peter Starne to the cookout, hoping to reconnect him to some lively company and laughter. In fact, she had made a point to stop at the desk on her way out and had asked if someone from the facility would be willing to bring him.

"I'll see what I can work out," the red-haired young woman behind the desk told her. "He's such a sweet old fellow, I'd love to see him have some fun instead of staying in his room reading all the time."

By the time her guests started to arrive in steady numbers, borrowed lawn chairs and folding tables were ready. The grills were heating up, giving up fragrant smoke in preparation for the hamburgers, pork chops, and hot dogs. A table full of appetizers and drinks waited for anyone who cared to partake. To give the party a more authentic feel, Western swing music played on a CD player.

On the porch, Alice had arranged pieces of Princessa

jewelry in such a way as to show off the delicate beauty or
dramatic flair of each one. Inside, she displayed Divine Décor
to demonstrate how various pieces could enhance a room. In
the parlor, on two borrowed long library tables, Alice's cookies, pies, cakes, and other treats had been carefully pack-
aged, ready for sale. A huge honor jar had been set up in the
center of one of the tables, and buyers contributed what they
felt was a fair price for baked goods that they chose to have.

Annie crossed her fingers that this party would not
only bring together and enhance the community, but that
it would give Alice a respite from financial worry for a
while. She prayed it would also kick off fresh interest in
the woman's businesses.

At one point, Annie stood on the top step of her shady
front porch and watched her visitors mingle. She listened
to their laughter and lively conversations, knowing that this
brainstorm had been one of the best ideas she'd ever had.

At the west end of the porch, where Alice had arranged
her jewelry, Stella Brickson browsed through the necklaces.
She picked up one, a delicate gold chain that held a single
teardrop-shaped amethyst pendant. Annie walked over.

"Isn't that lovely?" Annie said. "Look how it catches the
light."

Stella held it up higher, tipping her head to one side and
watching the light hit the stone.

"Yes, it's beautiful. I've been looking for something like
this—" She broke off as she focused on something beyond
the porch. Annie followed her gaze and saw Papa Dexter
getting out of a vintage panel wagon, complete with wooden
side-panels and an external visor above the windshield.

Stella laid the necklace aside and rushed into the house.

Annie's mouth flew open, and then she hurried in after the older woman.

"Stella Brickson!" she said, finding her in the kitchen filling a glass with water from the tap. Stella drank deeply, and then set the glass down with a little gasp of breath. "What on earth! Are you afraid of Papa Dexter?"

Stella glared at her. "Of course not! That's the most foolish question you've ever asked, Annie Dawson."

"Well, something is going on. If you aren't afraid of him, then you surely dislike him a lot. Why?"

Stella started to speak, stopped, started and stopped again.

"Annie, too many years have gone by, and I am far too old to be dating." She uttered the word with the same emotion with which she would have uttered "stealing."

"Dating? You mean you and Papa have gone out?"

"No! I just said I am too old for that sort of nonsense."

Annie stared at her, and then burst into laughter. Stella glared.

"Oh, Stella, are you too old to have fun? To enjoy dinner or a movie? Or a nice drive?"

"No, but ..."

"No buts. Just because Papa Dexter is interested in you—as a woman—does not mean you have to run off and marry him tomorrow. It doesn't even mean you have to kiss him or hold hands. What are you afraid of, that he'll ask you to the prom or to go steady?"

Stella blinked at her. "I ... I ... I don't know! Oh goodness!" She got another glass of water and drank half of it.

"Annie, do you know how long it has been since I've been out with a man?"

"Too long, I'm thinking. Nothing has to happen that you don't want to happen, Stella. And from what I know of Papa Dexter, he's a sweet fellow. He's not going to make any unreasonable demands."

Stella drew herself up straight and composed her face, though her pink cheeks might remain rosy for a while.

"I suppose you're right, Annie. I really haven't given the matter a lot of thought beyond recognizing that a woman my age has no business chasing after a man."

"You aren't chasing, Stella. My stars! You are running, as fast as you can, like a scared rabbit."

The older woman's mouth flew open. "I am not a scared rabbit!"

Annie lifted one eyebrow skeptically.

"Prove it," she said. "Go out there and talk to him. Be friendly, be courteous, and if he asks you on a date, for heaven's sake, go for it! Unless you're too afraid."

"All right, Annie Dawson. If for no other reason than to prove to you I am not afraid, I'll go talk to Alexander Dexter." And she marched right out of the kitchen, down the hallway, through the front door and outside. Annie followed with a smile, but then she stopped dead in her tracks.

Is that what I've been doing with Ian? she thought. *Have I been so scared of appearing to be chasing a man that I've been running like a scared rabbit?* As Annie stood on the porch of Grey Gables, she saw Ian Butler, the ubiquitous mayor of Stony Point, helping with the barbecue—her barbecue and her party. She thought of the praise Grady had heaped upon her—how she had moved on in her life with courage and conviction. Ian caught her gaze and returned it warmly. *Maybe I haven't moved on as well as Grady imagined,* she thought. She vowed she would try, in the future, to stop running like a scared rabbit. She waved a warm greeting to Ian, who returned it with enthusiasm.

Later, while mingling with her guests, Annie found herself grabbed and hugged. When the hugger pulled back and let go, Annie was looking into the face of Alice MacFarlane.

"Annie, this is the best party ever! I've already sold some jewelry, several pieces of Divine Décor, and more cookies than I can count. Oh, and that barbecue smells heavenly. Thank you! Thank you for being such a great friend!"

"I'm happy it's going so well, Alice!"

"It looks like everyone in Stony Point is here," Alice said, looking around. Then she stopped with her gaze fixed. "But I don't think those two are from Stony Point," she said, nodding her head toward the end of the driveway. "At least I've never seen them. He is a dish, a dreamboat and a hunk."

Annie turned to look.

Grady Brooks was strolling up the walkway with a lovely dark-haired woman on his arm. The way he was looking at his companion removed all doubt as to how he felt about her.

"It's Grady," she murmured to Alice.

"Are you kidding?" Alice almost shouted in outrage. "With another woman at his side? I thought you and he were an item!"

Annie gave her an exasperated look. "Oh, hush that kind of talk. We were an item only in your matchingmaking little head," she said. "Excuse me. I need to greet them."

"Annie!" Grady called as she approached with a big smile.

"I'm so glad you could make it, Grady!" she said, giving him a quick hug. She turned to the woman. "And this must be Chris?"

"This is Chris," Grady said proudly.

She shook hands warmly with Annie. "It's so nice finally to meet you. Grady has told me so much about you, Annie. And please, let me thank you for giving him whatever nudge you gave him."

"I'm glad to have done it," Annie said, laughing, "whatever it was. Grady, are you going to tell me now?"

He smiled and gave a little nod.

"I think now is a good time. Long ago, I lost Chris because I was afraid. Afraid I couldn't succeed in a serious relationship; afraid I couldn't provide for us the way I wanted to; afraid I couldn't make her happy. When Chris got in touch with me a few months ago, I was afraid of disappointing her a second time."

Goodness, Annie thought. *I've been around a lot of fear lately.* There had been Alice's fear of losing her business, her own fear of letting go of the past, Stella's fear of living fully in her old age, and Peter Starne's fear of letting go of his guilt.

"Somehow, reconnecting with you, Annie," Grady continued, "has recharged my batteries. As I told you the other day, you never let change or fear of the unknown stop you. I needed that boost, and you gave it to me." He grinned largely and slipped his arm around the woman's slim shoulders. "Chris and I are getting married!"

She lifted her left hand and wriggled her fingers so the diamonds of her new ring caught the light.

"That's right. And I'm moving to Arkansas to become first lady of Cooper City."

Annie clapped her hands, laughing in delight. "Oh, I am so happy for you both! This is wonderful news."

Chris leaned forward and placed a soft kiss on Annie's cheek.

"Thank you," she said softly.

"I'm glad I was able to help." She indicated the milling crowd, the chairs, the displays, and the food. "Let me introduce you to some folks, and please feel free to mingle. You'll find us Stony Pointers a friendly bunch. Whatever you do—please eat! We have more food than you can shake a stick at."

Annie was making her way through the crowd an hour or so later when her eyes fell on the bright red hair of the young woman from Seaside Hills Assisted Living. She was seated next to Peter Starne in a patch of shade near the front porch. He was gazing at the crowd, his expression curious, cautious, and yet somehow bright. The young woman was smiling warmly at him as he talked to her.

"Mr. Starne!" Annie exclaimed, approaching him with her hand out. He reached up and grasped it. "I am so happy you could come."

"I haven't stopped thinking about what you said. Then Joy here kept encouraging me to come today, and I decided to make some changes. Do you think ninety-four is too old to make changes?"

Annie laughed and squeezed his hand before letting go.

"Not at all! Joy, thanks for your help. Now, can I get either of you anything to eat or drink?"

"I don't want anything just yet," Joy said.

"I believe I'll just sit here and watch everyone for a while," he said with a smile. "But thank you, Annie. You need to play hostess to your other guests now. Looks like you have a lot of them."

Later, when the afternoon had worn down, Ian, Wally, and Mike Malone pushed the piano out onto the front porch. She and Jason stood on the top step, and she called for everyone's attention.

"We have a special treat today," she said. "I think you all know Jason." She threw him a smile. "We know he can drive Stella Brickson all over Stony Point quite well, but did you know he can play the piano beautifully? Well, today he's going to give us a mini-concert."

As he walked behind her to the piano, he muttered, "I hope I don't mess up too badly." He seated himself with a confidence that belied his words, drew in a deep breath, and began to play with as much grace and skill as any concert pianist Annie had ever heard. He played a variety of music, from The Maple Leaf Rag to Amazing Grace to Rhapsody in Blue.

When he finished to thunderous applause, Annie gave him a hug and said, "Jason, you have found your second calling."

Just as the men were about to move the piano back into the house, someone called from the crowd. "Annie! Can you have them leave the piano outside a little longer?" The red-haired young woman approached, Peter Starne leaning heavily on her arm.

"Would it be all right if Mr. Starne plays something for you?"

Her heart swelled.

"Oh, yes! That would be lovely."

She raced down the steps and walked on his other side, helping Joy to steady his climb up the porch stairs.

As Joy settled him on the piano bench, Annie said to the curious onlookers, "We have another brilliant musician in our midst today. Some of you know him, but for those who do not, Mr. Peter Starne, Stony Point's favorite piano tuner, will share his talent with us. Mr. Starne, the stage is yours."

The audience murmured and applauded. The old man smiled at them, bowed his head graciously, turned to the keyboard and flexed his fingers. Within the few notes, Annie recognized the sonata he had written for Olivia. The light, melancholy tone hushed the crowd as they listened, enraptured. When he reached the part where the music had ended on the handwritten score, the chords changed and the melody took on an even sweeter sound, a tune that caused tears to sting Annie's eyes.

She gazed at the composer—the man who had so long ago borne such hope and promise, and then had buried so much of himself in regret and pain. As Annie watched, it seemed that the years fell away. She could almost feel the presence of Olivia—ultimately Peter Starne's first and only true love—as if the young woman had been watching, listening, and loving the sonata that was, at long last, finished.